A Capital's Perils

Adventures on Brad Book 8

by

Tao Wong

Copyright

Tao Wong

A Starlit Publishing Book

Published by Starlit Publishing

PO Box 30035

High Park PO

Toronto, ON

M6P 3K0

Canada

www.starlitpublishing.com

E-book ISBN: 9781990491382

Paperback ISBN: 9781990491399

Books in the
Adventures on Brad series

Contents

Chapter 1

The creator of this level of the Dungeon was sick. Very, very sick in the head. So much so that if Daniel had a chance, he would certainly make use of his Gift to heal them. That was the only way that Daniel could imagine they would have come up with the rotating, pink-and-white-colored swirling walls that made up this level.

Every step of the way through the Dungeon, they had to fight a sense of vertigo and nausea. The sickly-sweet aroma crept through the tightest silk weave, burrowing into the senses such that all you could smell or taste was the perfumed odor, the licorice candy taste on their tongue. The floor sucked at their feet, refusing to let them go, even as the walls turned in a circular fashion. Until the floor finally released, and forced the Adventurers to tumble to the new "floor," their skin and flesh and armor enmeshed in the cloying environment once more.

And the monsters.

The monsters were just as nightmarish.

First were the Candy Hoppers—tiny, toadlike creatures whose natural camouflage made them almost impossible to see against the candy-colored pink and white swirl of the walls and ceilings. They sank their needle-like feet into the ground, allowing them to hold on even when the entire room rotated. When their prey came close enough, they would jump. Upon contact, they would swell, multiplying in size and drowning the poor target in toffee if they managed to surround the head. Of course, they only tripled their size, so if an Adventurer managed to get a hand or shield or sword in the way, they would only have a large, urn-sized ball of toffee impeding them. Even then, blocking was the preferred tactic, other than dodging the attacks entirely.

Except, of course, the Candy Hoppers were smart. Smart enough to only launch themselves in small numbers, such that once an Adventurer was trapped by the first, the second and third waves could impact the head or chest. Suffocating the victim to death.

There was nothing that Daniel's Gift could do if an individual suffocated to death. In the short term, he could stop the body from dying.

But without air, the decline was guaranteed, and no magic, no matter how powerful, could fix that.

Even so, the Candy Hoppers were not that horrible to deal with. They were fast, numerous, and only damageable via magical equipment. But anyone who managed to make it to the lower level of an Advanced Dungeon had magic equipment galore.

No, the second major monster type that inhabited the Dungeon was the real danger. Unlike the ambush predators of the Candy Hoppers, the Colossal Headcrunchers were sweet golems. The base form easily shattered under any sharp-edged strike, but they reformed from the ground. To destroy them, you had to locate their golem core, which was tricky since it was in a different location for each Headcruncher.

Other variants had sticky, toffee-like Headcrunchers that did not shatter but instead sucked up blunt and sharp strikes with equal ease. Only carefully placed attacks could lop off pieces, allowing blade wielders like Omrak to slowly whittle the monster down.

And then were the true Headcrunchers, the aged, base variants that refused to shatter and moved like rolling boulders. Those spun down turning rooms, often picking up speed with their Skills and caroming down long corridors in unpredictable trajectories. Spearwalls were useless; only towering shields with **Momentum Nullification** enchantments could protect the group. That or a **Sonic Wall**, cast by Lady Nyssa.

Lastly, of course, were the long-range dangers—in this case, mushroom candy variants. There were two kinds—the first, an exploding spore variant that choked those that were caught in the explosion and left them with a poisoned status as well as attracting more monsters to the group. And a second, more painful variant that fired needles of hardened candy canes at anything that neared.

All in all, fighting through the final level of Porthos in Silverstone was a pain and a half. The repair and washing bills were expensive, the mental and physical fatigue of crossing multiple levels building up and driving the team to distraction.

But the rewards . . . the rewards were well worth it.

For at the present moment, for Daniel Chai, the final goal stood waiting before him. The door to the Final Boss chamber, the monster that would mark themselves as full Advanced Adventurers, worthy of a Blue-colored badge.

Nearly a year of alternating Dungeons, of fighting and grinding to increase their resources, buying new equipment and delving nearly every day had resulted in this. Finally, finally, they were here.

***

The Adventurer-cum-healer turned to his friends, his gaze flicking over the group to begin his final assessment. The necessity of this procedure had been long engrained into him as de facto leader and main source of healing. His **Healing Aura** had been working overtime for the last twenty minutes on everyone since their last battle, helping to increase their base regeneration, but he knew that at the first level, the changes were minor.

First were the front-line fighters. Omrak, son of Losin, stood fully kitted out. Gone—so long gone that Daniel could barely remember him—was the shirtless Northerner. Shirtless because his clothing kept getting destroyed, not due to any particular preference to be naked. Now, Omrak wore a fully enchanted, soft leather armor piece that had self-regeneration and impact-resistant enchantments on them. Metal gauntlets covered his hands, generating a subtle but powerful lightning aura that channeled itself through his two-handed greatsword. The weapon itself was new, a drop from the floor below, and had a **Bleed** effect on it that was, amusingly, useless on these floors. Under his open-faced metal helm, Omrak grinned back at Daniel, still excited at the prospect of the delve.

Beside the large Adventurer stood their other front-line fighter. Carrying a newly purchased **Momentum-Nullification**-enchanted tower shield, Zef the Lizardkin stood at the ready, his trusty spear over his shoulder, the light green patina of his scales glistening through the cracks of drying candy. Like Omrak, he wore light leather armor, his racial skill **Scales of the Dragon** offering him more than sufficient protection against most attacks. Behind, his tail lay on the floor, offering the big Drake a third balance point. While he had complained initially of being forced to use the shield, he had taken to the new mode of defense with an alacrity that made Daniel doubt he would ever give it up, even after this Dungeon.

Behind the pair of front-line fighters were the ranged party members. Anne, their archer and secondary healer stood, a simple metal breastplate covering her chest while hardened leather pieces were placed across the rest of her body. The mixed leather and metal suit was in actuality a full set, enchanted to offer both protection and, most importantly to the smaller Adventurer, speed. Strapped across one side of her body was her war quiver, arrows at the ready, while the tiny skullcap that protected her head was set at a jaunty angle.

Charles, Lady Nyssa's bodyguard, was their team's secondary archer. He wore a full set of plate mail, much like Daniel, though his showed the battering of ages. Still, the magic that the suit of armor had been inscribed with decades ago still powered the armor without issue, both negating the noise of his movement as well as allowing the bodyguard a three-hundred-and-sixty-degree sense of the surroundings. It made him an exemplary bodyguard, a fact that was all too necessary as they journeyed deeper into the Dungeon and ambushes became more commonplace.

Especially since the Lady Nyssa, their only Mage, had yet to learn to pay attention to the surroundings. At least, not as much as she should have. It was only the careful tending of her bodyguard and the numerous enchanted accessories that she carried and her magical robes that kept her safe. She had everything, from a **Major Necklace of Deflection** to a **Ring of Misdirection** and a **Bracelet of Emergency Healing** on-hand. Never mind the pair of wands that she used for attack and her own spells. She was, to Daniels's chagrin, not readying herself but chewing on a portion of their latest kill, the broken toffee orb a part of their loot that she had claimed.

The toffee golem orbs, once the Headcrunchers were slain, were the major loot of these levels. These orbs only lasted anywhere from a week to a month, but during that time produced a small but regular amount of the sweet substance. Since sugar, in any form, was rare and expensive and required a shipment from outside the borders of Brad, the Porthos sugar orbs were highly prized. There were, of course, two other Dungeons in Brad that produced such spoils, but one only via the Floor Chest in a Beginner Dungeon and the other, a consumable drink in an Advanced Dungeon.

Beside the oblivious Lady Nyssa was Asin, the Catkin crouched on the tips of her toes, a wand in hand which she waved down her furred body. Of them all, the Catkin was the one to suffer the most on these levels. The sugary substance stuck to her fur, matted it and, when she fell, had a tendency to pull hair out. The wand that the light leather–wearing Catkin was using on her body helped to allay some of those effects, layering an oily substance across her fur and helping it regrow.

It still meant that she had the occasional bare patch of skin showing through, a factor that made the Catkin more than a little upset and embarrassed. Still, the money they earned from running the level kept the complaints from the greedy Catkin to a minimum.

Having made his assessment on the team's readiness, Daniel nodded to himself. Still, he raised his voice to call out and confirm. "Everyone ready?"

"Yes."

"Yup."

"Aye, Friend Daniel!"

Confirmations rolled in from the group, and Daniel smiled. He pulled the visor of his helmet down, feeling the weighty clunk, and checked that it was locked in place before he hefted his hammer. The summoning enchantment of the hammer was all too useful to leave behind, especially since he had paid for a boost to it. But, like his friends, he too had enchanted his armor. His, unlike many others, gave him an additional spell to wield and a Mana store, giving rise to the name of his plate mail—**Armor of the Healer**. It still seemed pretentious since the Mana in the armor was good for only a single cast of the **Heal: Major Wounds** spell, but since Daniel could cast through the armor, he was not about to complain.

"Then let's finish this."

Omrak put his hand on the door and pushed. The door to the Dungeon Boss chamber rolled open, leaving the group to step in and face the challenge they had been building towards for months.

Chapter 2

The inside of the boss chamber was somewhat less insanely designed, lacking the kaleidoscope coloring and swirls of the current walls and chambers before it. The basic structure, exemplified in the ceiling and floor of the chamber, mimicked the look of a confectioner's kitchen. Or at least, what to Daniel seemed to be a typical confectioner's kitchen, with multiple tables, the series of ovens, cooling racks, and storage bins. In truth, Daniel had never been to a confectioner's shop, and so he assumed it was similar. In either case, floor and ceiling were all made in what he assumed to be normal wood.

The confectioner himself, the Confectioner King, was a rural town individual whose hands were filled with sticky toffee that he massaged. He barely even looked up when the team streamed in. It was well known that he did not start fights, though those attempting to attack him from outside the boss room often generated even more problems for themselves. Among other things, monsters would swarm the corridor while its rotations would increase. The longer the Adventurer stayed outside, the faster the corridor would rotate, eventually throwing

Adventurers around and then drowning them in the increasingly liquid and sticky walls.

It was for this reason the team made sure to step within the room as a group before spreading out, readying themselves to begin to fight. Daniel eyed the other walls, which, unlike the wooden ceilings and floors, were made out of the strange, candy-like substance of the exterior walls. Those were a trap for the Adventurer teams that took too long to take down the Confectioner King.

Daniel held up his hand, counting down from three as they readied themselves to begin the fight. Asin raised and clenched her hand, signaling the archers to release the first volley of the battle.

The team did not bother to imbue their attacks with any special skills, for immediately, the Confectioner King's special defenses sprang into place. Pans rose up; little moving slimes of sweetness jumped out, intercepting the arrows. Even the thrown **Fan of Knives** by Asin, who'd snuck around an angle, was blocked, this time more actively by the king himself. The goopy wave of toffee absorbed her attacks, even as small electric sparks ran along the substance, hardening and making portions of it flake off.

Of course, the archers were only the first wave of attacks. Lady Nyssa was weaving a powerful, sonic attack at the moment, hands moving in arcane motions, even as Omrak strode forwards, his big greatsword swinging and ready to shatter the tables, stools, and other furnishings in the room. Next to him, Daniel was doing the same at an angle that would not take him close to the Confectioner King.

Only Zef was staying behind, his job to protect the Mage. At the last battle of the Dungeon, she would not be holding back, and as such would be the primary damage dealer. The rest of the team would continue to attack the king and the various furnishings within, for the entire room was a trap.

This was proven to both Asin and Daniel a moment later, as the furniture moved and launched their attacks. Asin had to throw herself into a flip, dodging over the suddenly moving metal trolley that had previously been used to move trays of sweets around. Daniel contended with a swarm of tiny, splayed hand-sized sugar slimes. The toffee-like, sticky creatures swarmed the plate mail-wearing Adventurer, attempting to pull him to the ground. He, in turn, swung his weapon, batting them aside with ease, his skill in blunt weapons having grown. Those few slimes that he missed striking were blocked by his shield, though that was less than ideal as the creatures stuck to it, weighing down his defense, while slowly creeping upwards.

In the meantime, Omrak finally arrived near the Confectioner King. He swung his greatsword, his reach so great that he bypassed the table that sat between the pair of them. The king did not even try to dodge Omrak however, instead thrusting his hands outwards as he sent a wave of toffee at the large northerner. Just before Omrak's blade would hit the Confectioner King, he was pushed backwards as the table between them lurched forwards and knocked him away. A moment later, the toffee struck his upper body, enveloping him and quickly hardening. Small tendrils of smoke began to appear across his armor, floating upwards as the acid within the toffee ate away at his defenses.

The Confectioner King's defenses were not entirely perfect, as Anne's trick arrow, fired up high and then dropping almost directly downwards, bypassed the swarming furniture. It plunged deep into the Boss's arm, drawing a howl from the florid monster. Meanwhile, every single arrow by the bodyguard continued to be blocked, though the slimes that intercepted the arrows grew slower, the poison within the arrows overwhelming their defenses.

Daniel, noticing his friend's predicament, quickly scurried over to Omrak and then struck his toffee-covering. His first attack sent cracks running through the hardened sugar net and also elicited a grunt from Omrak. Ignoring the pain he was causing, Daniel swung away, attempting to free his friend, even as Asin bounced around the room, dodging living furniture.

"Jobs!" the captain growled out, upset.

Daniel understood; his job was to destroy the furniture. But Omrak was stuck. With a heave, the Northerner shattered the cracked toffee, growling out, "Go."

Daniel scrambled away, idly noting that Zef was casting his spear to destroy moving fridges and warming racks, before beckoning it back with his **Return** skill. It just added another layer of chaos to the fight.

The next few seconds were hectic for the team as they dealt with the monsters, and the occasional blast of sticky toffee, forcing them to be dodge or be drenched. Every other minute, the Confectioner King would bring his hands down onto the table, and more tiny slimes would spawn. Those that were not destroyed would sometimes group up, growing larger.

As the group scrambled around, Lady Nyssa finally finished her spell. The glowing orb in her hand shot towards the center of the ceiling, hanging in midair. It let off a shrieking wind that set the team's teeth on edge, even through the protective enchantments that they all wore. However, the majority of the spell was focused, shaped to target the slimes and their king.

Slowly, the vibrations from the sonic cone built up, the slimes resonating to the high-pitched sound. The creatures lost control, and even the Confectioner King took damage, his eyes, nose, and ears beginning to bleed.

Angered, he clapped his hands together.

The next stage of the battle began, the entire room rotating. Floor became walls, and the team tumbled towards the sticky toffee that had liquefied, threatening to stem the movements of those who could not stop. In this case, that included the majority of the team.

Only Asin managed to stay clear of the new floor. Asin, hung off one of the moving cupboards, dodging its attacks even as she threw her knives at the boss. Anne, on the other hand, had released a series of roped arrows that helped attach herself to the ceiling and floor, suspending herself off the new ground.

The rest of the team tumbled onto the moving, sticky ground. Their armor began to smoke immediately, the mild acid eating away at clothing and skin. Luckily, the team had applied a resistance potion to all their equipment beforehand, knowing what was to come

Even as the team struggled back onto their feet, Daniel could not help but grin. Lady Nyssa's spell was doing much greater damage than they had expected. Without the ability to defend against the sonic attack, the Confectioner King was helpless. The rest of this fight was going to be a straight-up slugfest.

***

Omrak roared, lightning blasting out from the red aura that encompassed his form. The attack made the red light around his body disappear even as the Confectioner King froze, his body shocked still. In the midst of the creature's shock, Zef's spear came through the air, plunging into the king's body and skewering it through one side entirely. As the Boss staggered away, Asin jumped on it, her knife glowing as she used **Penetrate** to plunge the blade deep into the monster's head.

Daniel, a step behind, raised his hand to strike at the monster. However, he never managed to strike the Boss for it burst into white light, its body disappearing as it dispersed. A purple Mana crystal fell from its body, bouncing off the ground, the crystal the size of Daniel's closed fist. It was the largest and brightest crystal he had ever seen, and he gulped a little as he grabbed at it.

Only for it to be snatched away by Asin, who was cradling the crystal, eyes large, yellow pupils gleaming as she held the crystal to her. Daniel snorted, straightening, and eyed the group. He started casting **Healer's Mark** immediately, watching as Anne did the same on Charles. There was not much damage to heal though, the pair having worked to keep the team healed during the fight. In truth, their team was luxurious in having a pair of Healers in it compared to so many other groups.

"You are going to let us see that, yes?" Lady Nyssa said, the Mage looking less than pristine for once. She was wiping—ineffectually—at the toffee that stuck itself to her body and hair, but she never took her eyes off the crystal.

"Yes. I've never seen one so large!" Anne said, landing on the goopy floor after a moment. She had cut herself free, leaving the arrows behind as she strode over to Asin. "I bet none of us have!"

"I have." Charles, the normally silent bodyguard offered. Everyone turned to him while he shrugged. "I have accompanied the Lady's father on certain errands before."

"Oh, right." There were nods all around.

"But I have never held one that was mine," he continued, his voice hinting at a little avarice in it.

"Oooh, you almost have a personality there," Daniel teased, before gesturing at Asin, who reluctantly handed the stone over. The moment she did, she scrambled over to the Dungeon Clear chest that had appeared, eyes wide with excitement.

Zef, surprisingly, followed along with her, less interested in the Mana stone than the equipment. Even Omrak crowded Daniel as he handed the stone away reluctantly, allowing everyone to grip it. He did have to ask though.

"Have you not held one?" Daniel said to Lady Nyssa.

"No. These are not commonly used, even by noble houses. Craftsmen perhaps, but my family is not . . . well, of that bent," she said, her eyes tracking the Mana stone that was now held in Anne's hands.

"What kind of bent are they?" Daniel said, curious.

"We're Mages and Adventurers, mostly. Some members join the King's army, but there's not much opportunity there so they mostly stay as Adventurers if they are so inclined," Lady Nyssa explained. "We hold to the old traditions."

Beside her, Charles nodded in agreement.

Daniel mentally translated her last statement to the political realities he was fast learning. Old, traditional families were the least powerful—politically—in the current regime, with their members generally fewer in number due to losses and dedicated to the cleansing of

Dungeons. That allowed more politically motivated and land-and-merchant-heavy noble houses to control the royal court.

Not that the royals themselves were under control, but influenced. After all, they could not hold off the enemies on the borders—the Orcs being the most prominent—by themselves and needed the aid of the noble houses. If nothing else, to pay for the Royal Army.

"Beautiful," Lady Nyssa breathed out, holding the Mana stone up to the light. Daniel chuckled but moved away, leaving the others to watch over the stone as he walked over to check on what they had acquired from the treasure chest.

Perhaps he might even find an upgrade to his hammer for once.

Chapter 3

There was no upgrade, at least for him. The floorboards had provided the stone, and the chest had provided a total of four different enchanted objects. That had been a little disappointing. The rules of loot in Dungeons were that the more enchanted objects that there were, the less powerful each enchantment was. Thankfully, that degree of disappointment was somewhat belayed by the appearance of a rare enchanted accessory.

The Necklace of Aiming was not a particularly powerful, but the passive boost it provided to thrown and loosed objects meant that it was always in demand. Accessories were much rarer, especially since anyone could and would wear them. Of course, with Anne in play, there was very little doubt that it would go to her. However, to Daniel's surprise, she declined to take it immediately and left it with Asin.

The next enchanted object were braces, which were a nice relief. Not only were they sized such that the majority of the group could wear them—barring Omrak—the braces also had the ability to give a skill and a Skill Proficiency. That the Skill Proficiency was in lock picking was about the only negative of the bracers.

The next enchanted object was a simple pouch, though the inscription involved was easy to pick up. It was an enchanted pouch of anti-pickpocketing, where its mouth would not open except for the individual who had linked to it initially. It was not entirely desirable since the pouch was missing the antitheft option of alerting the owner if the entire pouch was taken. Those were almost always present with more expensive pouches. Even so, this would keep slippery fingers from stealing what was within. However, for Adventurers with the **Inventory** Skill Proficiency, such pouches were almost entirely useless. Only nobles and rich merchants would pick up something like this.

Lastly, the final item was a single crossbow bolt. The black-fletched, black-bodied bolt was an unusual item, with an extra wide broadhead tip. It was a Crossbow Bolt of Finding, allowing the attacker to fire and forget the weapon. Since the crossbow bolt was enchanted with durability, it was also extremely difficult to break, ensuring that it was reusable afterwards. Obviously, they were not as popular as an actual Crossbow of Finding, but the enchantment that affected the crossbow bolt by itself was generally more powerful.

Once everyone had picked up their armor and equipment, and cleaned themselves off as best as they could, the team exited the Dungeon by the simple exit portal. There was nothing else to do, at least for today. Rather than, of course, selling the loot and celebrating.

***

It was later that evening, seated in the Seven Stones Guild's guildhall, that the group met once more. What followed, were hours of being fêted by the other members of the guild, as their clearing of the final floor of Porthos cemented the team as one of the elite groups in the guild. At least, for Silverstone.

Even Gadi, the stuffy vice-guildmaster, managed to unwind enough to share a couple of drinks. He left soon after, knowing that his presence would stifle the celebrations. That and the fact that the guildmaster had once more disappeared, leaving the poor man to deal with the numerous bureaucratic issues that running a guild created.

It was only relating to the celebration, when the majority of the other Adventurers had trooped off—most to sleep and rest, a new passion for clearing floors burning within them—that the team sat together, and Anne leveled a bombshell.

"I'll be leaving the team now," Anne said, her voice low and shy. The once over-excited teenager had calmed down in the last year of Adventuring with the group, as the burdens of healing and exposure to a world outside of Adventurers and Dungeon delving at hospices matured her.

"What? Why?" Omrak grumbled, pounding his fist on the table.

"I was offered a place on another team. Vice-Guildmaster Gadi spoke to me about it, just before the run. I've been considering leaving, even before that," Anne said.

Daniel nodded, having guessed some of that before. While he was not extremely close to the archer, due to their roles and his own position as a more senior healer, the pair spoke often. They had even, briefly, considered a dalliance, before pressures and good sense drove the thought out of both their heads.

Lady Nyssa, always socially astute, noticed Daniel's lack of surprise. "You knew?"

Daniel shrugged.

"I expected that might happen. Anne is needed in other parties. As a certified Healer, the spells and aid would make delving much easier," Charles said.

Anne nodded, turning her hand sideways a little. "Like to try my hand in a new team, the healer." She shot a glance at Daniel, a little shy.

The healer could only nod, offering her his congratulations and assurances of support. He understood, since in many ways she would always play second fiddle to him if she stayed. While she might, eventually, become a more powerful traditional Healer, his Gift would always make him better.

His Gift . . . it always made life complicated. The ability to heal, almost any injury, was extremely powerful. Of course, it also came with a price, as decreed by Eralis. In this case, the price being his memories. Which was why, comparatively, he would always be a lower level than his friends. His life experiences, torn away with every use of his Gift.

"Bah!" Omrak said out loud, looking disappointed. "Now we will have to break in another archer."

"No sad, leave?" Asin said, poking her blonde friend in the side.

"You are right. She's going on to something bigger and better than us."

"Not bigger. Just different," Anne defended herself.

"Definitely not better," Lady Nyssa said, tilting her chin up. Then she relaxed and smiled at Anne. "I am glad though, that you have your own party. That is the correct step for your career."

Daniel nodded, then fear struck him. He looked around the group, meeting everyone's eyes before he asked the question that plagued him. "Is anyone else leaving now?"

"No," Zef said. "I could not ask for a better team." He glanced over at Asin, and then at Daniel, his unspoken concern clear to Daniel. After all, the skin always receives the worst treatment.

The others were quick to agree with Zef's sentiment, making Daniel relax. While he did miss the time when it was just the three of them, he had grown used to the new team. Though, a small part of him noted that Lady Nyssa and Charles were likely to leave at some point. When they found a better team, or their noble house sent for them.

"Let us toast our last night with Anne," Zef said, waving his scaled hand around until the server came by. Soon, the table was laden with even more alcohol, and the poor healer was being forced to quaff drinks.

By his side, Daniel could not help but smile a little. All things changed, and at least this wasn't a bad change.

***

Ever since the attacks and his joining of the guild, Daniel had chosen to stay in the guildhall itself. It did not have that many rooms available, even in such a large building, but for the most gifted healer, accommodations were made. Accommodations were always made for him, a fact that Daniel sometimes felt guilty about. Still, he was not guilty enough to stop making use of the large, single room that he had been assigned.

This morning, Daniel was dealing with a minor headache, one that was easily dealt with by a spell, and his own Status Screen. After the defeat of the boss monster, he had noticed that he had leveled up at some point during the fight itself. Probably, when he was killing one of the slimes. He had been quite close, just before he entered the room.

Now, without a headache, or a celebration to look forward to, Daniel could spend some time reviewing the Status Screen and decide what to do with his Skill Proficiency point. He opened his own screen, content to review the changes over the last year.

Name: Daniel Chai (Advanced Rank Adventurer)	Race: Human (Male)
Class: Level 26 Adventurer (11.6%)	Sub-classes: Level 6 (Miner) (12.1%)
Life: 360	Stamina: 360
Mana: 262	
Attributes	
Strength: 41	Agility: 35
Constitution: 44	Intelligence: 40
Willpower: 34	Luck: 22
Skills	
Unarmed Combat (Novice): Level 4 (183/100)	Clubs (Skilled): Level 4 (98/100)
Archery: Level 6 (32/100)	Shield (Skilled): Level 3 (43/100)
Dodge (Novice): Level 9 (54/100)	Combat Sense (Skilled): Level 6 (98/100)
Perception (Novice): Level 8 (13/100)	Mining: Level 5 (13/100)
Healing (Skilled): Level 6 (42/100)	Herb Lore: Level 6 (45/100)

Stealth: Level 3 (43/100)	Cooking: Level 5 (08/100)
Singing: Level 2 (31/100)	Tactics (Novice): Level 3 (18/100)
Heavy Armor: Level 5 (78/100)	Politics: Level 6 (71/100)
Sense Motive: Level 4 (83/100)	Leadership: Level 8 (83/100)
Skill Proficiencies	
Double Strike (III)	Shield Bash
Perin's Blow	Find Weakness (II)
Mapping (II)	Inventory (Adventurer Special)
Personal Armor (I)	Healing Aura
Flawless Dodge	
Spells	
Minor Healing (II)	Healer's Mark (II)
Cleanse (Toxins) (I)	Cleanse (Disease) (I)
Healing: Medium Wounds (I)	
Gifts	
Martyr's Touch—The caster may heal oneself or others by touch and concentration, sacrificing a portion of his life to do so. Cost varies depending on the extent of the injuries healed.	

The year of training had seen a huge difference for Daniel. The resources that the

Guild was willing to pour into him were significant, with the upgrades to his healing spells being the most prominent of all. Dedicated teachers would provide Daniel lessons at the hospice, allowing him to grasp and cast the **Cleanse** spells within the first few months of training. He had been on the cusp of learning those normally anyway, so that result had not been surprising.

Less useful in the Dungeon, but still desirable to have.

The **Heal: Medium Wounds** spell on the other hand was the one that the Guild had dedicated the majority of their time to having Daniel learn. That had taken a lot of time to study though, since he had to upgrade his base skill in healing. Translating knowledge that he gained intuitively via his Gift to book learning had been a minor struggle.

Then, learning the various spells forms and keeping them in mind while casting the spell had taken even longer. Even now, Daniel could only cast the spell via touch, but with the armor that he had been provided, he now had the full assortment of healing spells a full Dungeon-bound healer was expected to have.

Oh, there were other, more powerful healing spells. **Healing Word** for example was a fast-cast spell that magically regenerated wounds and, if there was any spell energy left, ran a "heal over time" effect on others. **Regeneration** and it's more powerful variant **Regeneration: Major** were extremely popular as well, since they replaced minor limbs or organs. They could heal wounds, of course, but the Mana to healing ratio for the **Regeneration** spells lent themselves to only selective use.

Daniel knew that there were other healing spells of course. Some groups made do with semi-direct healing aids, using things like a **Land Guardian's Healing Berry** or **Drink of Vitality** to provide methods of regeneration for teams. But, as a spell casting healer, Daniel's next most important spell was upgrading his **Minor Healing** to an area effect level.

That, unfortunately, required either a dedication of Skill Proficiencies or time to study. He was close to achieving the minimum Skill levels, but the area effect only began when you reached the fifth level. Speaking with Vice-Guildmaster Gadi, the pair had agreed that Daniel should attempt to study and learn the fourth level by himself, thus allowing him to dedicate a Skill Proficiency directly to the Spell when he next leveled.

That, however, was some time away. Being able to assess multiple individuals and warp a spell to work for groups at a time—and not target monsters or enemies—required high levels of not just the healing skill but perception. Also, some skill points in Tactics could help.

In truth, Daniel was more intent on **Healing Aura**. That had become an option a few levels ago when his Leadership skill had reached the appropriate level. His Tactics skill had long ago passed the minimum required, but Leadership as a skill set had not begun leveling till the Guild Trainer had helped him gain his first Level.

It was weird how some skills did not level until certain preconditions were met, but it was the way of the world. Scholars who had the time and curiosity could care about such things. For

Adventurers, they just did the best they could, working with Guild Trainers and the like to trigger or bypass necessary requirements.

Still, at least he had it now. It was a rare skill since it required three different skills to acquire, but Daniel reviewed the details on the Skill Proficiency with a grin.

Healing Aura

The healer is a paragon of leadership, one who cares greatly about his comrades. Those in a party with the healer or within a ten-foot radius and allied with him receive a trivial increase to their regeneration.

Skill Type: Passive

Cost: N/A

Effect: Increase base regeneration by 5%

A five percent increase to regeneration was, in many ways, trivial when one was Dungeon delving. The **Healing Aura** skill was more often taken and used by Medical Directors of larger clinics or even the Director of Healing for the Royal Army. A base increase to a clinic by the

Medical Director as he worked in his office could see a faster turnaround of all residents and decrease the number of sick days the healers and their assistants required. Even saving them from using a precious Skill Proficiency point on a skill like **Immune System Boost (Personal)**.

It was an uncommon Skill Proficiency to take when one was a Dungeon delver. However, the reason Daniel chose it was due to the upgrades. In particular, the fifth one.

Healing Aura (V)

The healer is a paragon of leadership, one who cares greatly about his comrades. Those in a party with the healer or within a fifty-foot radius and allied with him receive a major increase to their regeneration and other healing effects.

Skill Type: Passive

Cost: N/A

Effect: Increase base regeneration by 25%. Bleeding effects reduce in 200% of the time. Pain resistances increased by 50%. Disease and other toxin resistances increased by 50%.

Unfortunately, **Healing Aura** was a full Skill Proficiency, and as such, could not be raised in any other way than via Skill Proficiency points. Still, the fifth-level base increases were powerful and tempting.

As for his other Skills, most had lagged behind. Rather than attempt to learn a new Skill Proficiency, Daniel had leaned upon his first one—**Double Strike**. At the third level, it was actually a multi-strike ability that allowed him to chain up to four different strikes for minimal damage increases and drop-off in accuracy or fewer but more powerful, enhanced attacks. He could, if he timed it right, even slip in **Perin's Blow** or a **Shield Bash** into the final attack, offering him increased flexibility.

The use of a few, but upgraded, Skill Proficiencies was something that the Guild Trainer had recommended for Daniel. Rather than take the time studying and integrating a wide variety of Skill Proficiencies and attacks, he was better off focusing. Especially since Daniel spent less than half the time on the training grounds that dedicated fighters did.

It was a choice that Daniel agreed with, which was why he had gone ahead with the recommendation. It was also why he was considering adding another point directly to it, since a fourth level would increase the number of strikes possible by one and the amount of damage each strike did too. It would have been particularly useful fighting swarm creatures like the slime.

His attributes were somewhat similar. Due to his role as both a damage dealer and healer, he had ended up splitting his points in a consistent way, only ignoring Luck for the most part. Increased Intelligence gave him a better ability to comprehend Mana and a bigger Mana pool, while the need for a high Willpower was well known among all Adventurers. Not only did it decrease the number of mental issues, there were Dungeons where there were attribute minimums for Willpower. While some Dungeons had them for things like Agility or Constitution due to Dungeon layouts or environmental conditions, they were much rarer and were generally acceptable to bypass minimums via enchanted objects.

Not so with Willpower.

A lost Willpower-enchanted object could lead to the mental control of an individual and the loss of the entire team. Or having an Adventurer freeze, unable to move while crawling through a constricted route Dungeon, forcing his party to starve to death behind them.

As for his other physical attributes, Daniel kept them high to keep up with the rest of the monsters they fought. The current build plan he had had him maxing out on Agility at fifty, since anything more would be considered overdone. That would allow him to deal with the majority of monsters in the Advanced stage, with only a rare few too fast for him to handle.

For those, he had been advised to leave to his friends. And buy some area enchantment spells.

Knowing that, Daniel leaned towards Agility for his next block investment. It would leave him with only a few points left to the next stage, and his Constitution with his new armor was sufficient to keep him alive—a very important aspect of being a healer. Especially with his own little Gift.

Though, that did nothing to answer what he should do with his Skill Proficiency. He dismissed any more attack Skills, leaving him with either enhancing **Perin's Blow**—a powerful knockback skill that was useful against larger opponents—or his **Find Weakness (II)** Skill Proficiency. That would allow him, with his combined Leadership skill, to intuitively share his findings with others. It would be a nagging burst of knowledge, a whispered hint. Yet it could provide a bonus to those fighting.

The new Skill upgrade would see immediate upgrades to their fighting style. But it would, in time, fall by the wayside again unless he dedicated more points to it in the future as they faced more and more powerful enemies.

Whereas if he upgraded the **Healing Aura** ability, he would see little in terms of the team's current ability—though he was sure those staying in the guildhall would appreciate the increase—but it could benefit them all in the future when he got it up to the fifth tier.

Biting his lip, Daniel debated his options.
And finally, made his decision.

Chapter 4

A day later, the group reconvened at the guildhall. Most were cradling headaches, ones which Daniel was unkind enough to inform them they had to deal with on their own. He was scheduled to do a series of healing sessions with nobles and other groups that had paid for the privilege later that day, and as such had to conserve his mana.

The guildhall living room was somewhat subdued in the middle of the day, as the majority of Adventurers were busy in the Dungeons and running other quests. The only individuals within were trainees, taking a quick break, and other parties in between runs. Most, though, found other places to hang out, leaving the expansive dining room hall relatively empty.

"Are we sure we need another archer?" said Zef. He gestured over to Charles, continuing, "We already have one, I have my spear, all ruckus hatchets, and even Daniel contributes."

"Only until they realize he can't hit anything," Omrak said, grinning.

Daniel rolled his eyes at the ribbing, though he took no real offense. After all, even after so long, he still had trouble hitting the bullseye on a stationary target, never mind the monsters they faced.

"Seriously, do we need another?" Daniel said, frowning. "I recall being forced to deal with those Orcs in Aramis. That was not much fun, having to run through arrows."

"Adding another dedicated archer would help. Charles isn't exactly, well . . ." Omrak looked over to the bodyguard, who smiled.

"I understand. My Skills Proficiencies are more focused in the medium range. What few I have for long-range attacks are combined with my other attacks, like **Unerring Strike**," Charles said. "Even Anne had more Skill Proficiencies."

"Right. And if he realized something, even a single good archer could make a big difference," Daniel said. "If anything, we are a little lopsided as a team."

"And what are you saying? That we should perhaps training more Skills?" Lady Nyssa crossed her arms over her chest, glaring at Daniel. "I'm not going to use my Skill Proficiencies on that. And even if I learned how to use the crossbow bolt better, none of us would be able to trade our positions."

"No one is saying that," Zef replied.

The group slowly nodded, though left unsaid was the loss of loot. The more people in a group, the more they shared their earnings. Already, the team was quite large, bigger than any optimal number. Most teams averaged around five, though there were advantages to having large numbers. For one thing, they could tear through the Dungeon faster, in general. And of course, some teams had even more members, though they only fielded five or six at a time, due to injuries.

"Gadi?" Asin said. The Catkin, as usual, cut through all the talking, getting right to the point. In this case, the best person to inquire about a new team member.

"We should probably find them," Daniel said in agreement. He knew which team members were free. The Guild constantly churned through new recruits, and even if they weren't local Adventurers, Gadi would at least have an idea of someone else. And if not, he might know someone who wasn't part of the Guild but in the city who might want to join their team. They were one of the fastest improving teams in the city.

Or at least they were, though how much that would change with Anne gone was up to fate.

Daniel stood up, looking around. "Anyone want to join me?"

Asin shook her head. "Repair."

Lady Nyssa, however, among all the others who declined to deal with the bureaucracy, agreed. Daniel raised an eyebrow in surprise, before she clarified. "I have to speak with him about some other matters."

Nodding, Daniel led them upwards, to his office. Not surprisingly, the vice-guildmaster was seated behind his desk, handling the paperwork that his boss constantly put off.

"What can I do for you two? It's rare to see you grace my office," he said the moment they walked in.

"An archer," Daniel said, getting right to the point. He didn't think he needed to go into further detail, not with the vice-guildmaster.

"Yes. Unfortunately, I don't think there's anyone suitable in town," Gadi said.

Before Daniel could add anything, the guildmaster held his hand up. He shuffled his papers around for a bit, before finding a letter and tossing it over to the Lady Nyssa. The heavy-weight paper fluttered through the air, catching an errant drift and almost falling before the woman caught it, forced to take a couple of steps forward. She peered at the sealed letter, frowning at the seal, one that Daniel did not recognize.

"But I don't think it really matters anyway."

Daniel frowned before asking, "Why?"

"Because we've received a request that you journey to the capital itself," Gadi said. He inclined his head towards the sealed letter. "She might have more information than that. All I received, all we received, was a demand that you make your way there with your team as soon as possible."

Gadi's words made Daniel's stomach drop, as worries held long in the background came rushing to the fore. It seemed news of his Gift had finally made its way to the royal capital. And with it, his life had changed once more.

***

News of their impending journey jolted the team from their stupor. Lady Nyssa, reading through her letter, was forced to explain the issue to those less politically connected. Which, in their case, was pretty much everyone else on the team.

"Daniel's Gift is now a known quantity, as well as the Three Skills' action. The fallout from that caused quite a few shifts in the political web, which is why the guild has attempted to keep us out of it for the year. However, things have settled down enough that it seems they are willing to bring Daniel to the capital." A slight pause, as Lady Nyssa tapped the letter.

"What?" Daniel said, impatiently.

"It's just a rumor. But there's belief that the King's youngest son is looking to join a non-royal team."

"Why would he do that?" Zef asked, frowning. "That's dangerous."

"He's well known to be rather fool-hardy and stubborn. He doesn't like being 'coddled' as he puts it."

"Can I trade places with him?" Zef said, grinning. "I could do with some coddling."

Asin snorted and poked Zef in the side with a clawed finger. He laughed, shifting away only slightly. It wouldn't bother him much, not with his scales and his Skill Proficiencies. Even Charles had grinned a little at Zef's joke, though he had kept silent.

"I think it is admirable that he desires to win glory for himself!" Omrak rumbled.

"You would." Lady Nyssa rolled her eyes. "If the rumors are true, having a Gifted healer like Daniel might well draw him to the Guild."

"Politics," Asin snarled, her tail lashing out behind her. She crossed her arms, looking truly unhappy.

"It is the capital. It's all politics," Lady Nyssa replied.

"More importantly, what kind of Dungeons are there to run in the capital?" Daniel asked.

Everyone turned to look at the Lady Nyssa, the only one of the group to have gone to the capital. Or so they assumed. She in turn looked at Charles, who straightened. "The capital has two Master Class Dungeons, the reason for its development. In addition, it has also a single Advanced Class Dungeon as well, though the Advanced Class Dungeon is actually a sprawling Labyrinth type that accommodates four times as many Adventurers as normal."

"No Beginner Dungeons?" Daniel said, curiously.

"No. There are four within a day's ride of the capital though, most in smaller towns and a village. In two days' ride, there are two more Advanced Dungeons that are available for use too," Charles said.

The group frowned a little, with Asin scowling. She spoke, giving voice to everyone's thoughts. "Unusual."

"Yes, it very much is." Charles nodded. "The entire region is considered a high Mana flow location and highly unusual. Though, it's not surprising that most other capitals on the continent are in similar locales."

There were nods all around. Controlling Dungeons, especially Master Class Dungeons, was important. They were what gave birth to powerful Master Class Adventurers after all, which were individuals that could make significant differences in war efforts.

"So when do we leave, Friend Daniel?" Omrak rumbled.

"I . . ." Daniel frowned, thinking over the message. "'As soon as possible' was the request. I guess in a few days?"

"Quest?" Asin growled.

"What kind of quest do you think we could get?" Lady Nyssa sniffed.

"Escort Quests of course," Zef said. "Good thinking, Asin."

"We're on a timeline here!" Lady Nyssa said.

"And we need money," Zef said. "Or at least, I'd like it. A good caravan escort can be fast and profitable."

"If there is one," Lady Nyssa snapped.

"Enough," Daniel said, raising his voice. "No use arguing. We'll check the boards first, and if there is one that works—in terms of speed and when it leaves—we'll take it. If not, we'll travel without." He paused, then Daniel rubbed his nose. "Or at least I will. You guys could come slower?"

Asin let out a chuff, her tail lashing idly. Zef, by the side, snorted, and Omrak voiced his disapproval. Lady Nyssa obviously intended to be with him anyway, so there was no need for her to speak. And Charles was always with her.

Holding his hand up to ward off their disapproval, Daniel nodded. "Fine. We're agreed, then. We'll travel together and deal with the quest if it comes up."

Lady Nyssa's eyes narrowed as she realized she'd been tricked into agreeing, but she kept her mouth shut. Daniel, smiling a little to himself, stood up.

"I'll check it out now." Immediately, Asin popped up, happy to follow along. Charles, at his employer's command, joined the pair as they headed out to the Adventurers Hall.

It was time to move again. And if Daniel had a flash of sadness at that thought, of never having roots, it was gone soon after as he looked forward to the next city, the next Dungeon, the next adventure.

Because that's what Adventurers did.

Chapter 5

The trip to the capital took the team just over three months, including multiple stops along the way at cities and towns. The group joined two different caravans on the way, working as caravan guards as they travelled through the countryside. The presence of monsters in the wilderlands was a given, though constant patrols and Adventurers kept the numbers to a minimum. More dangerous were the occasional bandit groups that preyed on travelers or, when they were close to the border, Orc raiding parties.

For all the dangers of travel, none of it was ever particularly dangerous for the team. As Advanced Adventurers, they were more than suited for the relatively safe ground that they were traveling through. Even the single Orc raiding party had been defeated with minimal loss of life, only a single unlucky caravan guard catching a crossbow bolt through the eye during the initial clash. A well-placed **Sonic Cone** by Lady Nyssa had disrupted the Orc's charge and afterwards, a flurry of crossbow and bow attacks forced the Orcs to keep their disjointed arrival.

Thrice along the way, the team delved into Dungeons that they came across. Twice were simple Beginner Dungeons that they blew through, collecting the Boss Chest at the end for the enchanted equipment. The trip added a ring of Mana for Lady Nyssa and an enchanted knife and sheath that returned the thrown weapon after a few seconds which was given to Asin. The other equipment was resold, padding the team's pockets. As for the last Dungeon, an Advanced Dungeon, the team only managed to make it three quarters through the expansive, desert biome before they were forced to leave and continue their journey.

In the end, it was a road-weary team that arrived at the capital gates. The gates themselves were only the first of many that the team would need to pass through, with the capital built in a strange-at-first-glance fashion for those who did not know its history or the necessities of building around Dungeons. Once you understood the Dungeons though, the layout of the entire sprawling city made sense.

First, any sensible, civil-government-built walls to contain a Dungeon. Beginner Dungeons might find their walls skipped—like in Karlak—where the possibility of a Dungeon Break was extremely low. Add the simple expedience of easy-to-emplace blocks and most Beginner Dungeons received minimal defenses.

On the other hand, even the Advanced Dungeons in a place like Silverstone were blocked off. Guards at the main entrances were at the minimum, with additional walls like the ones that formed around Arthos added along the way. Concerns of a Dungeon Break were always predominant, though pressures of civil governance occasionally saw the walls taken down, especially in heavily trafficked Dungeons. Even Advanced Dungeons were unlikely to see a break if they were constantly cleared.

However, Master Class Dungeons always had walls around them. Not only was the historical precedent of insufficient Master Class teams to clear a Dungeon well set, the speed that a Master Class Dungeon could overwhelm the local guard force and militia was such that walls were necessary. No local militia could hope to stop them on open ground and even with enchanted walls; they could only slow them down long enough for the army and Adventurers to arrive.

So walls went up around Master Class Dungeons always. Depending on the size of the Dungeon, you might even have a second set, though an inner bailey and an exterior, larger wall set that encompassed the Adventurers Hall and other localised merchants and suppliers were more common. Amusingly enough, Daniel knew that even with the added danger of a Dungeon Break, the cost of leasing locations within the walls were extremely high due to the higher income of Adventurers in general.

In any case, that was the first set of walls in the city. Those around each of the Master Class Dungeons and, yes, the Advanced Class Dungeon. Those walls encompassed a larger area, just due to the lower threat level and the higher number of Adventurers that made their livelihoods there.

Then, a second set of walls. This was built between and around the civilian buildings, the residences and shops of the civilians who grew up around Dungeons. As communal resources that provided a significant number of resources, Dungeons always saw the presence of civilians who were there to serve the Adventurers, civilians who then needed services for themselves. At first, of course, they would grow up around each Dungeon, and since the Master Class Dungeons were set miles apart, it was easier to serve the Dungeon surroundings themselves rather than a middle location. And because the surroundings were—initially— dangerous, walls were needed. City walls, to safeguard themselves.

Then, of course, there was the royal castle. That had been built on the hill overlooking the Dungeons themselves. The castle with its curtain walls and the local noble houses below it, all of which had to be guarded, which meant curtain walls for the royal mile and then another set of walls for the noble quarters. And then, when the servants and other suppliers grew up, a third wall for those individuals.

Farmers had taken to working the land between each of these sprawling villages turned towns at first, but they too built their own walls. Eventually, when the number of farmers and the growing towns had linked up, it was decided that a single, larger wall was required. Which resulted in a much more significant project, one that was supposed to take into account the future.

And thus, another wall was built. This one towered above all the other, smaller works beforehand. Easily over fifty feet tall, crafted from black obsidian, the working a mixture of magic and highly Skilled Builders, the Black Wall encompassed all three Dungeons, their towns, the royal castle and the noble quarters and their town, and the farms that fed them all.

Then, of course, at a certain point, the land within had been all used up as enterprising nobles bought up land for their farmers, smart merchants built up residences and buildings for the common people, and the city grew again.

What seemed like enough space became too little for there was no more free land.

And the city sprawled again. Which resulted in the very walls that Daniel stared at now, a shorter, twenty-foot stone-and-mortar construction whose creation was more of a statement of where the city began than an actual impediment.

City of a Hundred Walls indeed.

***

"Name?"

"Daniel Chai. Advanced Adventurer." Daniel held out his Adventurer Card, smiling a little at being able to say that. He lost his smile a moment later, when he was forced to hand over the silver piece. The caravan master had let the team loose the day before, not wanting to pay for their entrance fees. Not that Daniel minded that much.

It was just a silver. And if they had journeyed with the caravan, they would still be getting ready. And behind the team, the morning traffic into the city was already queuing up, and the sun had barely broken the horizon.

"A whole Ba'al silver!" Omrak grumbled, hands crossed once he was through. He looked even less than impressed but froze along with Daniel when they heard the guard speak.

"That's not enough. It's a gold for your kind," the guard was saying to Asin and Zef who had tried to hand over their silver.

"What? That's outrageous. They just paid a silver," Zef said, his tail curling up near his body now. Asin's ears had flattened even as she looked around, the nearby guards on high alert now.

Daniel, turning, spotted even one of the guards cranking back on a crossbow, though he had yet to insert a bolt.

"What's going on here?" Lady Nyssa called out, pushing up to the pair. She glared at the guard, as if he was no more than a bug.

"And you are?" the guard said.

"Lady Nyssa Mazur, of House Mazur." She held up her card. "An Advanced Class

Adventurer. Like the rest of my party. This is my bodyguard, Sir Charles Moffat."

"Lady Nyssa," the guard bowed a little, not even taking her card but only glancing at it. "My apologies. But these creatures are refusing to pay the entrance and warrant fee."

"Warrant fee?" Lady Nyssa said, frowning.

"Yes. It's a fee introduced to pay for the bounty hunters to serve the warrant for their arrest." When Asin let out a low growl, he continued to explain. "For when they break the law."

"Not criminal," Asin snarled.

"Yet," the guard said, sniffing.

"I know nothing of this law. When did it appear? Do you have the announcement on hand?" Lady Nyssa said, holding a small hand out to Zef and Asin to calm them. Daniel, walking back idly, placed a hand on his hammer head, though he knew better than to draw. There was no winning this kind of issue with violence.

"It was published a year ago. And we have a copy within our offices." The guard gestured towards the small tower connected to the wall.

"If you wish, we can adjourn within. But the beasts aren't allowed into the city till they pay."

Lady Nyssa hesitated, looking to Daniel. He nodded to the noblewoman, who acceded to the request. With minimal complaints, both Asin and Zef stood to the side under watch of the guards, including the guard who had now loaded his crossbow. With a flick of his gaze, Omrak and Charles were sent to join the pair and keep things handled, while Daniel joined Lady Nyssa within to review the city ordinance.

Together, the pair stared at the document that was passed to them, reading through the scroll with bent heads. It was towards the end when they found a small codicil, one that had the noblewoman hesitating.

"I could but . . ." She frowned.

"You're worried?" Daniel said, aggrieved.

"Yes. About how they'd feel about it."

Daniel nodded, feeling a little ashamed of what he thought of her. She had not indicated fear of the pair breaking their word.

"We could ask them. I know Asin at least has the money but . . ."

"Prickly. Both of them."

Daniel could only nod, and the pair quickly exited. They found traffic having resumed moving, though the Adventuring team received more than a few looks. Even as Daniel walked closer, he watched as a farmer, rolling past the group, cleared his mouth and spat right near the Catkin and Lizardkin, both of whom had coldly indifferent looks on their faces.

"Friend Daniel, Hero Lady Nyssa, what word?" Omrak rumbled as the two closed.

"There's an exception. But it requires that I guarantee the good behaviour of our friends. In that case, they need only pay a silver," Lady Nyssa explained.

Zef stirred from his unmoving position while Asin's nose and muzzle curled up. Her whiskers twitched, but she stayed silent. It was Zef who spoke first. "A silver's good. I'm willing, if you are."

Lady Nyssa inclined her head, before the group looked at Asin. Who in the end made her answer known by stalking over to the guard and holding up a gold coin. She slapped it into his hand and waited for the guard to put the entrance pass on her Adventurers Card before she stalked in, wordlessly.

"Proud, isn't she?" The guard laughed a little, while Lady Nyssa acknowledged Zef's entrance under her aegis.

In the meantime, Daniel walked over to Asin to stand beside the silently fuming Catkin, her tail lashing out behind her in slow metronome.

"We're not in Karlak anymore, eh?"

To that, Asin could only let out a humorous chuff.

***

To start, the team made their way over to the Seven Stones Guild building in the capital. The group, led by Lady Nyssa traveled deeper into the capital with each step, headed for what was known as the Adventurers District. While the area within the immediate walls of the Dungeons were also Adventurer districts, those were often prefaced with the names of the Dungeons beforehand. The neighborhood they were going to was called such because of its location, between the three Dungeons, allowing the Adventurers easy access to it.

As they travelled, the group spied upon the capital city. In many ways, the city itself was familiar, with whitewashed and grey clay-and-mud buildings lining cobblestone streets everywhere. Often, retail shops were beneath the multi-storey buildings, some up to four stories high, with their ever-expanding floors shading those below. An interesting addition to the city, along with the addition of sewers, were the raised wooden platforms before each entrance to the retail stores, allowing pedestrians to walk in safety from the moving carriages and away from the open sewage below before it fell away into the sewers.

It led to a generally more sanitary city, though the much larger and more extensive sewer system beneath the city led to the over development of slimes and other sewage-eating monsters. It was the killing of these monsters and the small colonies of other semi-sapient creatures that lived in the warrens below that kept Beginner Adventurers busy in the capital. The entire capital was an ecosystem of Adventuring and Dungeon exploration, along with the rather unique Master Dungeon of Warmount. Or, more formally, the War of the Mountain.

That Dungeon was somewhat different, in that even Beginner and Advanced Adventurers could enter and advance themselves within the Dungeon. Like its namesake, the Dungeon was a war-based scenario, with an entire mountain and castle that the Adventurers had to defend replicated by the Dungeon. Beginner Adventurers were forced to run errands within the sprawling edifice, dealing with monster saboteurs and the never-ending replication of shadow creatures within the darker recesses of the building. Advanced Adventurers were tasked with holding the walls along with the multiple and varied simulacrum defenders, while Master Class Adventurers led the simulacrums to seek out enemy Champions to defeat and siege weapons to sabotage. To "win," the entire encounter required multiple groups of

Adventurers, all working together to shatter the backbone of the enemy army before driving them off.

All of which the team had gathered from rumors and stories told at the Adventurers Guilds on their way to the capital. Many Adventurers from outside the capital looked down upon the "capital" Adventurers, for many never left Warmount itself. They, in turn, looked down on the newcomers who came to challenge their Dungeons for their lack of "common" knowledge and their over abundance of caution.

It led to some degree of animosity, and Adventuring guilds that were capital-specific only. Of course, the Adventuring Guild itself kept an eye on the situation, making sure to keep the animosity and competitiveness to words for the most part.

Still, it did mean that non–capital-only guilds, outside of a few well-known examples, were relegated to the Adventuring District. Even if the other guilds had the funds to purchase a building within the inner walls of a Master Class Dungeon, they often found it impossible to do so. Sales of precious land within those districts were uncommon and often done via backdoor channels. By the time most guilds even learnt that such land was for sale, the sale would have been concluded.

And that did not even account for the ever-expanding influence of nobles in all that. Their political power along with the funds they could bring to bear, often in towns and Dungeons outside the capital, offered them a chance to purchase such land well beforehand.

It led to the current situation that the group was staring at. Instead of the sprawling mansion that the team was used to in Silverstone, the Seven Stones Guild building in Warmount was a pair of adjoining buildings connected to one another, barely three-quarters the width of the mansion in Silverstone and more horizontal than vertical. Looking up, Daniel could count a total of six major stories and a glimpse of potentially two more stories in a tower.

To Daniel's senses, he could sense the channel of Mana flowing through the building, enchantments to bolster the materials that held the building aloft and kept them from collapsing. These were not passive enchantments but active ones, energy poured into the building via Mana stones that were taken from the Dungeons.

An expensive proposition, but it allowed the guild to build upwards in the small amount of space they had been able to purchase. Even so, just from the flow of individuals entering and exiting the paired doors leading to the guild building, Daniel could tell it was insufficient for their needs.

"Well, I guess we're here," Daniel said eventually, looking at the group. There were short nods from all, Lady Nyssa the one looking most impatient. He understood her impatience, since she, unlike the others, had a place to go afterwards.

"Come on," Lady Nyssa said, deciding that the group had done enough gawking. Glaring at the trader who attempted to skirt around her, she strode in, followed closely by Charles.

Asin let out a little chuff and then strode forwards, ears swivelling as she took in the surroundings. The Catkin was on high alert, her tail waving behind her in short, sharp jerks. Zef followed, sticking close to his fellow Kin. The low number of Kin in the Capital was concerning, as was their initial reception. Rather than let his friends leave alone, Daniel hurried after, finger dropping down to his pouch where their letters of introduction were kept.

Time to see what the Capital was all about.

Chapter 6

"Hurry up and wait," Lady Nyssa grumbled, arms crossed under her breasts.

Charles flashed a quick smile, before his face smoothed out. The group were seated in an outdoor restaurant outside the Adventurers Guild, having not found a seat within the main building itself. The entire building was made up of multiple connected buildings, with each section dedicated to a different focus.

Having learnt their lesson in Silverstone, Daniel had acquired information about the building before they had travelled to it the next day, reporting in to the new Adventurers Guild and registering the completion of their escort quest. After being paid, the group had attempted to find a table within the Guild but all such tables had been already filled, forcing the team to reconvene outside in one of the many restaurants serving the overflowing numbers.

"Typical," Asin said.

"It is good!" Omrak rumbled. "I look forward to testing these new Dungeons. It is long since we have managed to pit our mettle against new foes worthy of our attention."

Zef snorted, his spear propped up beside the table. Rather than answer, he sipped on his drink of pressed grafa juice, a purple and green drink that had cost a single silver per cup. Daniel's eyes had bulged at the price, though Zef had paid it without a word. It seemed the grafa fruit was rare up here, but common where Zef's people were from originally further south.

"The royal family will speak with us when they wish," Daniel said with a shrug.

So would the guildmaster, it seemed, since neither had chosen to speak with him when they had reported in yesterday. In fact, this morning, they had already received a reply to indicate their presence in the Capital was acknowledged and that an appointment would be made for them.

At some point.

"Whatever." Lady Nyssa waved her hand. "Daniel, my uncle would like to speak with you at some point. He is the head of the household in Warmount and would seek to meet my team leader." Left unsaid was the other aspect of why he would like to see Daniel—his powerful Gift. That, by common agreement, was not going to be discussed in the capital unless they were under privacy wards.

"Of course. Till then, as Omrak says, we should look at delving." Daniel made a face as he stared at the remnants of their lunch. "Living here is going to be expensive."

The price for their meal had been thrice that of Silverstone, and Silverstone was already expensive. Even their accommodation had to be paid for in the guild itself.

"Day delve," Asin said. When the group looked at her for more explanation, she huffed and added, "Summons."

"Oh, right." Daniel nodded. It was definitely concerning if they received a summons and had to show up the next day and they were doing a multi-day delve.

"Oh, look at that kitty. It's even got a knife. I bet it thinks it's an Adventurer." A voice, raised, cut through the hubbub. As Zef and the rest of the team looked over, it continued. "And they've got a lizard too. I guess some people like strange pets."

Daniel turned, spotting the smartly dressed brunet of a man who was mocking the group. He was nudging his friends, all of them young men, all of them dressed like nobles. Daniel's eyes narrowed a little and he began to rise, only for Lady Nyssa to put a hand on his arm. She mouthed the word "don't" to him.

"Oooh, look. It seems the creatures have a master."

Asin let out a little chuff but shook her head and turned away from the taunting group. After a second, Zef followed her and focused on his drink.

"That's right, know your place."

"Why don't you go back to the sewers where you belong!" Daniel snapped, fed up. Lady Nyssa groaned, while Charles smoothed out his features immediately.

"You peasant dare to speak back to me? I'll have you whipped." The young man puffed his chest out. "If you don't know better, I am Rene deBone, the son of Marquise deBone."

"Obviously, he didn't lose his bone at the right time . . ." Zef muttered under his breath.

"What did you say, you lizard!?!" Rene almost screamed at Zef, stalking forwards.

Rather than let the other man touch his friend, Daniel stood up and interposed himself. Omrak followed suit, the young blond man looming over the friends who had accompanied. They sneered at Omrak and Daniel, their eyes raking over their common clothing.

"Newcomers. I hate newcomers. They never understand their places," one of the young men said, his voice with a little lisp as he spoke.

"We have done nothing to you. Just go away," Daniel growled, glaring at the youngster. The entire group was probably no more than sixteen, all hot-headed. Daniel idly noted that they all wore little copper armbands, a fashion statement he had noted on many others.

"Oh, now you learn caution. Well, forget it. I challenge you, as the master of those creatures, to a duel!"

Daniel paused, flummoxed. He turned away a little, to stare at Lady Nyssa. "What?" he mouthed. Before she could answer, the young man was screaming and shoving at Daniel.

"Don't you dare look away from me, peasant. I challenged you to a duel."

"I'm just . . . wait. You mean with swords and stuff?" Daniel said, shaking his head.

"Yes, a duel. Of honor. Or do you outcity peasants know nothing of that?"

Daniel sighed and tapped the hammer on his hip. "I don't really use a sword. So no."

Beside him, Lady Nyssa who had risen and moved forwards, winced. Still, she kept her mouth shut since he had already spoken.

"What? You can't turn me down." Rene looked a little thrown off by the refusal, but soon enough his face was growing red again.

"I think I just did."

"You, you, honorless dog . . . !"

"Adventurer Chai here is a healer," Lady Nyssa cut in before the boy could begin another full tirade. "And as such, he is well within his rights to decline the duel."

"A healer? Him?" The lisping noble spoke up, his gaze raking over the muscular and stout youth's form. He did not speak it out loud, obviously not wanting to gainsay the refined

Lady Nyssa, but his voice held all the doubt he could put in it.

"Yes, Lord . . . ?" Lady Nyssa replied.

Rene looked confused a little, his challenge interrupted. The lisping lord, eyeing Lady Nyssa and the silent Charles, who stood beside her in an obvious guard position, sketched a bow. "I am Lord Jean-Marc Halocene."

"Ah, Lord Halocene!" Lady Nyssa curtsied, which to Daniel seemed strange since she was in her adventuring gear which consisted—of course—of pants. Of course, for propriety's sake, she had a very loose skirt over her pants, but it had high slits to allow her the most freedom of movement. "I would like to extend my house's condolences on the death of your mother. She was well respected."

"Thank you." Lord Halocene returned her curtsy with a bow. "And you are . . . ?"

After Lady Nyssa introduced herself and Charles, the other nobles were forced to bow and offer their own names and stations. Rene had retreated a little, looking angry at having his challenge stymied by social pleasantries.

Once it was done, though, Lord Halocene cut in. "I'm surprised to see you with such . . . individuals."

"You know my house," Lady Nyssa said, shrugging one shoulder. "We must go where the delving takes us."

"Yes. You're one of those houses . . ." sneered Rene. Jean-Marc glared at his friend, giving a short shake of his head. Rene fought for composure, but eventually nodded his hand towards Lady Nyssa in apology.

"Come. If we don't go soon, we'll not be back for dinner," Jean-Marc said, gesturing towards his friends. The group streamed off, all but Rene, who stood there, frustrated. Eventually, the lord sneered again at Daniel, spat near where Asin and Zef sat, and stalked after the group.

Only when they had gone did Lady Nyssa relax, letting out a long exhalation of relief before she stiffened again and rounded on Daniel.

"You! I indicated you should not have reacted!"

"They were insulting Asin and Zef!"

"Of course they were. They're Kin." Lady Nyssa offered a nod to the pair along with an apologetic smile. "They will be insulted and looked down upon in Warmount. They know that. They knew better than to react. You, though . . . !"

"They're my friends." Daniel crossed his arms. "I will not see them treated like that."

"Then you shouldn't have brought them."

Daniel shook his head again, angry, but the Lady was done with him and walked back to the table and sat down. She picked up her glass of wine and sipped on it, purposely ignoring Daniel, who stood fuming. Eventually, the healer sat down too, where Asin leaned over and faux-whispered.

"Thank you."

Zef offered a nod too, at which point both received glares from Lady Nyssa. Omrak, having taken his own seat, grumbled.

"I helped too."

Zef grinned, clapping the big blond on the shoulder. "Bah! You were in my way. I could not see their faces when Lady Nyssa told them Daniel was a healer."

The group chuckled a little at that, but Daniel raised a finger. "So why am I exempt?"

"It's the same exemption that is given to healers for treating others. You can't be forced to duel or engage in other challenges as a healer." Lady Nyssa sighed. "Too few healers, too many hot-headed fools. When there wasn't a blanket exemption, too many nobles and others found ways around the earlier rule of not challenging healer treatment results."

Daniel nodded slowly, rubbing his nose. He knew that he could not be charged for treating others, no matter the outcome. It was an important point in law, due to the low number of healers. The only way a treatment result could be challenged was by another healer, and only in a jury of peers with a truthstone in use. There were still abuses, of course, but it was the best compromise to keep healers willing to test new treatment methods and not flee the country for other, safer locations.

"Mmm . . . so are we delving?" Omrak rumbled, leaning forwards. "I think we should at least check out the first level—"

"No, we should gather some information first. Reduce the likelihood of problems," Charles protested, cutting in.

Daniel chuckled, watching the group argue, but he could not help but glance back towards where the group of nobles had stalked off. And then at his friends. Somehow, he did not think their troubles were over. Not just yet.

Chapter 7

The sprawling Advanced Dungeon of Warmount was busy. Unlike most other Dungeons, the Labyrinth of Zulo had multiple entrances and exits. It also, unlike most Dungeons, closed itself once a month to shift its internal layout, such that every month new Adventuring Parties had to relearn and remap the insides. Since it was the middle of the month now, the Dungeon was at its peak of busyness, as the central Dungeon Boss had yet to be found, and the prize for being the first to defeat it had yet to be claimed. Once it was found and the prize claimed, the Dungeon would lose a certain amount of attractiveness, as the rewards would decrease. Until it shifted again, at which point the few brave mapping teams would enter once more, earning large sums of contribution points and gold from the Adventurers Guild for the risks they took. Until they were done though, few parties would attempt more than the outer ring of passages.

Since the entire Advanced Dungeon was a single, massive labyrinth, the concept of "Levels" or floors was thrown aside. Instead, Adventurers in the Capital tracked the "depth" that they were in the Dungeon by the number of turns they had made. The more turns one made, the deeper you were within. This was, of course, much more imprecise than Levels and as such, the number of deaths in the early part of a month were increased—especially for those teams unused to the environment.

Just as often, monsters altered and changed in the Labyrinth. Not to the same degree, of course, but unlike the two or three varieties that made up a floor, with a total of maybe thirty different monsters in a large, expansive Advanced Dungeon, the Labyrinth had something north of two hundred varieties. Only thirty or so would be showcased any month, but with so many varieties available, the exact mixture was constantly changing, leading to the increased danger.

"And that's why we're lucky to be here in the middle of the month," finished Lady Nyssa as they waited for their turn to enter. The group rolled their eyes a little, since most of the information she provided was well known. They had, after all, multiple months to familiarize themselves with such knowledge on the way to the capital.

"How bad is it this time?" Daniel said, curious.

"Mmm . . . no one has reached the Final Boss yet, or at least have not announced it," Charles said, cutting into the conversation. "Though rumor has it that there are a few groups that are close. More relevant to us, the first two dozen turns are considered only mildly dangerous."

"Good." Omrak grinned, tightening the straps on his bracers and pounding one fist into the palm of his hand. "It's about time we did something more than chase away the occasional wild animal."

The other Adventurers could not help but nod. Because it was the capital, the volume of dangerous animals near the capital itself were insignificant. The only concern were bandits and even then, the danger was extremely low. Some caravans did not even bother with guards when they did the local circuit, content to trust in the king's patrols and the constant traffic to keep animals and bandits away.

If not for the fact that the Adventurers Guild had put a stop to merchant's cheaping out on not paying for the leg of the journey, the team would likely have had to pay their own way in from the outer ring of cities. But that was a known issue and no caravan or merchant caravan could get away with that kind of penny pinching. Not under the eyes of the Adventurers Guild. And since they controlled the flow of Mana stones, no merchant dared get on their bad side.

Eventually, the team found themselves before the doors into the Advanced Dungeon. They handed over their cards at the guard's request, who scanned them over. The senior guardsman frowned at the group from under his flanged helmet and deep-set eyes, but Charles stepped in, showing the guards the map and the packet of information they had already purchased.

"Prepared are you." The guard's voice was hoarse, as if he desperately needed a drink. He eyed Charles. "You been here before, then?"

"Escorting another of House Nyssa, yes. A number of years ago, but I recall my experiences," Charles said.

Daniel was surprised, the older man rarely offering information about his past. He had even declined to discuss his past experiences at Warmount, staying silent. Perhaps he had considered the matter unimportant when they were so far away and the Dungeon a distant possibility.

"Go on then." The guard waved, and the group trooped in. Ready to tackle their very first Dungeon in Warmount.

***

They did not bother stopping at the entrance room, passing through the cramped quarters quickly. Even the magical teleportation that brought them to the entrance room—one of many starting points in the Dungeon—was a minor matter to the team. The Dungeon was kind enough to provide location sigils above the exit corridor which were always correct, so it took them only looking at the sigils and locating their position on the map before the team began moving.

In the corner of Daniel's eyes, the map that made up his **Mapping (II) Skill** began updating. At the next Level, Daniel knew, he could even extract the map he created onto parchment, a Skill that made it easy to replicate such information for others and that Explorers and Mapmakers the country over made good use of. Every single one of the first teams into the Dungeon also had at least one such member with the Skill Proficiency, but it was not one that Daniel had much care for.

"Grey slate bricks, effusive lighting rather than illusionary torches." Charles nodded as they passed their first turn. The team was on edge, ready for danger but not expecting any. Since they took so long to enter the Dungeon today, the first few turns were likely already swept clean by earlier teams. It was only in the latter turns where they could expect monsters to turn up.

"What monsters are we expecting again?" Omrak asked, frowning.

"He already said," Lady Nyssa snapped but the blond just shrugged.

"It's okay. We can expect a few monsters here. Stone Rats are common in the first few turns. Not very dangerous, but they attack in swarms. Holes along the side of the walls and the ground are where they come from. Air Sprites accompany them, growing bigger over the next dozen turns before they are replaced. Keep an eye on the ceiling. They have a tendency to stay there," Charles said, answering without even needing to refer to his notes. "Lastly, melee monsters are a mixture this time around. Insect Lurchers are six-legged monsters that lurch forward and attack with their mandibles and the pair of scythe arms they use. Be careful; their mandibles can shear off unarmored limbs. We'll find them in varying quantities, increasing as we go along. There's also a Shadow Stalker that appears later in the eight turns onwards that has been reported."

The group waited for Charles to explain, all of them eyeing the holes around. Yet Charles did not continue.

"Well?" Zef growled out, poking idly with the tip of his spear into one particularly large hole warily. When nothing made a noise, he moved on.

"There's no description of them. Shadow-bodied and mutating. They attack from the back and shadows, kill and fade. When they are killed, they disperse." Charles shrugged. "Watch the shadows."

"Mmm . . . as if that is easy," Daniel grumbled. There were always a dozen things to watch out for, and what made this Dungeon hard was that they literally had to watch all around. Then again, it was an Advanced Dungeon. Beginner Dungeons were marked not just for the Level of the monsters one faced, but the complexity and danger involved.

Soon enough, the group had made their requisite four turns, treading their way deeper into the Dungeon. Asin, ahead of the group, had stopped at the last turn—and in the Dungeon, a turn was often more marked by a change in design than physical turns—to await them.

"Enemies?" Omrak rumbled.

Surprisingly, Asin shook her head. She pointed down the way and tapped her nose. "Party."

"Ah . . ." Charles, taking the lead, held a hand out. "Let us wait then."

Asin nodded, squatting down and peering into the darkness. Her tail idly lashed out behind her while the team settled in for the other team to make a few more turns. There was no reason to hurry them, and you never knew how the other party might react.

Soon enough, the other moved far away enough that Asin was happy to take the lead again. She resolutely turned down one of the t-intersections the moment they reached it, leading the team deeper in. She was barely thirty feet in the new corridor when an angry yowl erupted from ahead of them.

The group took off, Zef and Omrak charging forwards while Daniel and Lady Nyssa followed after more warily. Charles had his bow nocked but was wary of firing the weapon in the Labyrinth. Arrows could travel quite a distance, and you never knew who might turn a corner.

It did not take them long to spot the issue. The Catkin was being swarmed by Stone Rats, dozens of them crawling and leaping at her. Their small fangs tore at her clothing and sparked as they interacted with her lightning aura, some of them shocked into stillness. Still, there were so many that the Catkin was being swarmed and her superior agility being overwhelmed.

Omrak let loose a primal shout, issuing the Challenge of the North to call them towards him. In the meantime, Zef swung his spear in long arcs at the charging swarm that detached themselves from Asin to attack the Northerner. Many were impaled, more were struck down by the paired throwing axes the Northerner chose to wield against his smaller opponents.

Left behind, Asin finished tearing apart a Stone Rat with her claws, bleeding from multiple shallow wounds. Daniel cast a quick gaze over her and then threw a **Healer's Mark** on the Catkin before he waded in, taking care to deal with the few Rats that had managed to shake off Omrak's challenge to attack Zef from behind.

"'Ware. Above!" Charles's call was followed by the twang of his bow. A Light Sprite was impaled against the ceiling, the tiny creatures that were descending caught before they could launch their surprise attack.

Lady Nyssa unleashed a **Sonic Cone** at the ceiling, shaking the ceiling tiles and causing a half-dozen of the Light Sprites to plummet to the ground, unnerved. Daniel swung his shield and hammer at them, crushing bodies as he crouched low.

A long minute of harried attacks later and the dispatch of a lone Insect Lurcher by Asin, the group was able to relax. Omrak had received a number of shallow wounds along his legs and across a bicep, while Asin had managed to heal up over the course of the fight. A simple application of poultices to Omrak and the group was ready to continue, intent on exploring the Dungeon further.

It seemed, as promised, the first few turns were truly not that dangerous.

Chapter 8

"Hold it there!" Daniel snarled, his glove off, his hand buried halfway in Lady Nyssa's body. He was doing something incredibly dumb right now, but it was the only way to save the half-bisected woman. Looming a bare three feet away from him, Omrak fought, swinging his greatswords in wide arcs as he parried the attacks of the carapaced, six-legged pincered creature with its trio of stingers that harried those attempting to circle around it.

Nearby, Zef was staggering upright after being battered aside into the wall. He reached sideways, extracting a healing potion and downing it, grunting harshly as the magic contained within the drink took effect and healed some of the cracked bones that surrounded his body. At the same time, he held his hand out, **Recalling** his spear to him. The moment it arrived in his hand, he ran forwards to aid Omrak.

The Northerner was blood red, his aura imbued with the rage and pain of the attacks that had struck him. He was bleeding freely, but none of the damage was life ending. Daniel's **Healing Aura** was doing its job too, but had limited effect in such a short time frame for the injuries his friends sported. Unlike the wound that Lady Nyssa sported, the poison from a stinger seeping through the wide wound where not one, but two stingers had struck her. If not for her **Emergency Healing** bracelet and other enchantments, she would have died already.

Behind, Charles was fighting with his bow and a drawn dagger, stabbing and fending off smaller versions of the Level Boss. He was buying time, rather than attempting to kill the creatures, his face stretched into a hard rictus.

Behind, offering a distraction and playing a deadly game of duck and hide, Asin danced among the self-coordinating stingers, dodging them by inches as she threw her daggers. Each weapon was imbued with the lightning of her bracers, giving her attacks a bite that they would lack otherwise. Occasionally, she would imbue her attack with **Penetration: Drill Attack**, an upgrade to her normal **Penetration** Skill that required more Stamina and Mana to use, but allowed even thrown attacks to pierce the thick shell—at least, if she hit a joint.

For all that, Daniel could not focus on the fight around him. He had a much more important battle in front of him: the one for Lady Nyssa's life. The poison ravaged her body, slowing down and truncating any healing that his **Aura** or potions could do. He had to **Cleanse Poison** first, but his spell was too low-level to deal with this pernicious poison. No, he had to do this the hard way.

Inside his mind, inside his soul, Daniel felt her body shift. Energy flooded her form from his, Erlis taking his memories in payment for providing her divine aid. Or his body stealing the energy of a life lived to charge his Gift. It was a matter of faith and religion which explanation you accepted.

For Daniel, more importantly, he had a job to do. Poisons to neutralize and pump out, torn veins and arteries to clamp shut with his healing energy to contain blood loss. A body that was going into shock and needed to keep warm, a heart that was stuttering from the damage done, a mind that reeled and desired to flee as pain flooded it.

He shut down nerves, clamped down blood vessels, stitched up torn wounds as the last of the poison had finished being neutralized. The human body could do much, fix much, though in many cases it was simpler to just remove the poison. Especially a necrotic one like this, where dead or dying cells were shed and discarded and then regrown.

It was not, to Lady Nyssa's later chagrin, his hardest healing attempt. The Champion so many years ago was closer to death. Hers just had the complication of a necrotic poison. It was not, however, particularly puzzling. Skin just had to be regrown and reattached to other, torn-open portions. Skin and muscles, manipulated by the same energy to reattach to each end. Organs, pierced, were regrown, damaged portions broken down for more energy and nutrients.

It was simple. Daniel had done this—in mostly smaller portions—a dozen times. And so, because there was a fight raging on around him, he looked around. And blinked for a brief moment as he turned his head—he could have sworn he saw a pair of eyes staring at the body and him. Yet when he turned back, it was gone.

A shake of his head, as he noted that together, Omrak and Zef were pushing the Level Boss back. Together, their strikes had managed to cripple one pincer. The monster, unable to hold the large limb up any longer, was hindered in its movement as it attempted to spin away from the increasingly accurate attacks the pair of fighters landed on it.

Behind, Asin had managed, somehow, to entangle the pair of stingers that had threatened her and then pin them together with her knives. She, in turn, was crouched astride both of them, duelling the last stinger as its entire body bobbed and weaved. It was an insane level of Agility, one that only a Catkin with her **Unerring Balance** ability could have pulled off.

Tearing his attention away, Daniel extracted his hand from Lady Nyssa's body. The Mage coughed, tried to sit up, and crumpled back down as Daniel pushed his bloody hand on her chest.

"Not yet. I'm not done," Daniel said. He focused deeper, pulling on his Mana now as he sent his Gift back away. Instead, he wove the skeins of his **Minor Healing II** spell, using the touch component so that he could keep the majority of the energy for healing. It pulsed through her body, the Mana of the spell weaving new skin and muscles together. He cast it once more, before he pushed away from her body, a wave of weariness dragging at him. "Done."

"Good . . ." Eyes clearer now, Lady Nyssa stood up, her hands forming the edges of her spell. "Out of the way!"

Reacting to the shout, the trio assaulting the monster threw themselves away from the creature. It reared up, surprised by the sudden change of pace, only to be struck by the focused assault of the **Sonic Cone** that Lady Nyssa released. It was physically battered aside, even as the noise dove deep into its muscles and organs, tearing at the attachments. Her face in a rictus of anger, blood dripping from mostly sealed wounds, the woman strode forwards, her attack channeled.

Daniel watched for a brief second before turning away, scooping up his hammer as he charged to the rear where Charles continued to hold off the remaining attackers. He would worry about her mental state later. Right now, there were monsters to end.

***

Tugging on the bandage, Daniel finished securing it to Charles's arm before he stood up and cast **Healer's Mark** on the man. He surveyed the group, nodding in approval as Omrak finished bandaging his own wounds around his leg. The team was fixed, or at least as well as they could be. That meant there was just one last thing to do, as Asin finished picking up the Mana stones from the ground.

"What was that thing!" Daniel hissed at Charles.

"Floor Boss."

"I know that," Daniel said, waving his hand around. "We're only a dozen 'turns' in. We shouldn't have faced something like that yet."

"I did say that the turns were a rough guide, did I not?" Charles said, levering himself up as he checked his quiver and began refilling it from his inventory. "It's why this is a Blue-ranked Advanced Dungeon. You never know what you might find."

"You could have told us about the monsters," rumbled Omrak.

"I did for a few levels up," Charles said, crossing his arms and sounding angry. "These weren't included."

"What do you mean, 'weren't included?'" Daniel said. "We're halfway through the month."

"That doesn't mean every portion of the Labyrinth has been checked. We must have wandered into one that isn't marked."

Daniel's lips thinned, but he pushed the irritation aside. It was not Charles's fault that they were caught out. They had been warned it was dangerous. It just shook him a little, how close they had come to losing Lady Nyssa. Any other team would have failed. Even if they had a poison counter—and he swore to spend more time studying the spell as well as purchasing some higher ranked **Cure Poison** potions—the damage by itself would have been enough to end her. It would have taken a Master Class Healer to keep her alive, otherwise, and even then, it would be touch and go.

"That's unimportant. We have something more important to consider," Lady Nyssa said, nodding to Asin, who had finished picking up the last of the Mana stones and was patting the pouch that held it all. The Catkin stored the pouch the next second while Lady Nyssa continued, "Do we continue or not?"

There was a long pause then as the group stared at one another. Zef limped over, clutching at his side where cracked bones were slowly healing. The noblewoman was looking pale, her chest covered in strips of bandages that slowly leaked blood even as the pulse of **Healer's Mark** disturbed the Mana atmosphere. Omrak was battered and bloody, though his wounds were fast-closing, his Skill Proficiency **Health for Energy** trading Stamina for increased healing. It was a Skill most tanks would use during battle, banking on Stamina potions and other Stamina regeneration skills to keep them standing. Omrak, having Daniel around, mostly used it after the battle to help fix non-life-threatening wounds after the battle.

All in all, the team was rather battered. But they had taken out the most dangerous threat over the next few turns already, which meant that they could search for one of the many Dungeon chests that lay dotted through the Labyrinth. Unlike most other Dungeons, there were no guarantees that the floor chest would be next to the Floor Boss, since they had a tendency to roam.

"Daniel?" Lady Nyssa called out, making the healer finish his considerations. He looked over the team once more, then decided.

"We rest for half an hour. Then we keep looking," Daniel said. "No deeper though, we'll keep sweeping in and around and then back."

Charles pursed his lips, looking a little unhappy with his decision but eventually nodding. Omrak slumped down one side, pulling a cloth out from his inventory to begin cleaning his blade while Zef sat backwards, leaning on his tail as he watched the sides. The rest of the group took their own places to rest, with Lady Nyssa making her way over to Daniel.

"Thank you," she said, touching his shoulder. "That . . . I never thought it would—it could—pierce my defences."

"Powerful Level Boss. It caught us all by surprise," Daniel said. He shook his head, remembering how the false wall had crumbled as the creature ran right through it to launch its attack on the middle of the party. Even Asin had been tricked, though the Catkin was now poking at the wall, intent on finding signs to ensure she never missed the trap again.

"Yes. Still, thank you. Again," Lady Nyssa said. Her voice dropped, continuing, "And if I can help with the Price . . ."

"You can't," Daniel said, cutting her off. Even if his team knew of his Gift, he had yet to explain the full details of his Price. He was still reluctant to do so, since it would also indicate the full extent of his Gift. That and . . . well . . .

a certain reluctance to trust instilled into him by his grandfather.

For now, at least, the Price he paid, the memories he lost, would be his secret.

Chapter 9

The group trudged out of the Dungeon entrance the worse for wear. Luckily, they had not met any more dire threats on their further exploration and even located the Floor Chest in their region, acquiring a large Mana stone and a dagger with a poison enchantment. It was only a mild enchantment, but good enough that most of the team were eyeing it. Of course, Asin had first dibs being their main knife wielder, but if she chose to give it up . . .

Unfortunately, on their way back, they had run into another Floor Boss. This one had been accompanied by its minions, forcing the team into a harried and tiring battle, even if none of them were in particular danger of death. Just injury.

Which was why Daniel was nursing a headache right now, his Mana nearly fully drained. Healing the team with a series of **Healer's Mark**'s kept them functional and would ensure they could start another delve in a few days, but it did leave him tired. Still, as he looked around in the fading twilight of the day, he spotted more than a few teams leaving with graver wounds.

For all that Daniel might complain about his Mana loss and the lack of healing he could do for his friends, most teams had to juggle injuries, progression, equipment maintenance and purchasing and delving timing. At the capital there were more healers available than other cities. It still did not make their services cheap, but those willing to purchase healing potions, or avail themselves of mundane healing, could do so. Even magical healing was available, for a price.

Foremost, they would just choose to enter the Dungeon with minimal injuries, moving through lower floors as they ground out additional income, taking fewer risks and slowing their progression. Some teams would only delve when they were fully healed, going in in the best state possible, and in the meantime training to make up the difference in timing and pushing deep when they entered.

In either case, the luxury of entering a Dungeon fully healed every single time and regularly was limited too. More and more of those teams would cluster around in the

Advanced levels, or as Master Class teams. In fact, there were nearly no Master Class teams who did not have a healer on board. Both the dangers that they faced regularly and the need for constant delving made teams without such an individual on-hand non-viable.

Musing on the vagaries of delving, the group made their way back to the Adventurers Hall. They stayed only long enough for Asin to sell their Mana stones, returning with the funds for them to distribute. The quick discussion between the group saw them divvying up the earned silver coins while reducing the amount that Asin received in return for her keeping the poison dagger. The Catkin waved them off as she decided to acquire a new sheath to fit her weapon and only accepted Zef's company.

Daniel bit his lip a little bit, watching them leave, but knew that they would be mostly fine. Even if their presence was unwanted, they were clearly Adventurers, and a little leeway was given because of that. In any case, they were likely headed to the Beastkin quarters, to rest with others of their kind. There is a level of comfort that they drew from being around one another, of not having to always be on guard, to be careful not to give offense. In that sense, Daniel knew he was privileged to have seen a little into the world. Both as Asin's friend, and as a healer, he had been given glimpses.

In the meantime, the rest of the team returned to the Seven Stones Guildhall to rest. Then he wanted to wash and recheck their bandages anyway, and it would be simpler to do at the guildhall than anywhere else. He would have to check out the local hospices soon, verify where the free clinics were so that he could ply his trade. Even if he was going to be careful about how much of his own Gift he would use, the mundane knowledge that he had gained as a healer could always be of use. And, as he stepped through the shadowed alleyways where homeless and parentless children slunk and hid within, he knew there were always those who could use his Gifts.

Unfortunately for Daniel, it was not long after he had settled himself in an anteroom to the kitchen and finished re-bandaging Omrak's injuries that word of his arrival and what he was doing spread through the Guild. Soon a small line had formed of people who "just wanted a quick word," people who were wondering if he "could just look at something quickly."

Before things could devolve, a matronly old lady came stomping down. Arms crossed, she prodded people with a sheathed dagger to make them move aside before she managed to make it to Daniel and glare at him. Dressed in a full, pale noblewoman's day dress, edged with lace and pink flowers, she still looked intimidating as she stood there, one foot tapping.

"What is this commotion?" Lady Marshall, the vice-guildmaster of the Seven Stones Guild of Warmount said.

"It's . . . well . . ." As she glared at him more, Daniel shook off the flash of fear and quickly explained what had happened.

"This impromptu crowding is entirely unsatisfactory," Lady Marshall grumbled. "However, the terms of your inclusion to the Guild did include instances of healing. You may carry on, but I *will* have order in this line." She turned and glared at the rowdy crowd who shrank from her and sorted themselves out into a line without a word. Nodding in satisfaction, she swept her gaze over Daniel, who was cleaning his hands in a basin of water, and the few bandages and other poultices he had laid out before landing on Omrak, who had stood up, stretching. "You!"

"Me?" Omrak said, blinking.

"Yes, you big lummox. Go to the healing station and pick up additional supplies for Healer Chai here. Then make sure the kitchens have enough boiled water. Got it?"

"Yes, but . . ."

"Good." Turning away, she stalked away back to her room, leaving a flummoxed Northerner to watch after her.

"But I don't know where the healing station is . . . !" Omrak wailed softly.

"Come on, big boy. I'll show you the way," a red-haired young lady, eyeing the tall drink of water, said, a lascivious grin crossing her face. Her hair was so dark red that it was almost brunette, and her eyes sparkled as she turned to

114

the bored Adventurer behind her. "You'll hold my place for me, right?"

"Yeah, yeah."

Grinning, she linked her arm with Omrak and dragged the man along, the Northerner looking rather hapless while Daniel chuckled. Then, turning back to Charles, who was next, gestured to the chair. "Well, sit. I'm going to need to check on that chest of yours."

Charles looked around at the rather open space before them before he shrugged and pulled his shirt off. "Perhaps some others might find a curtain or two? For the ladies, when their turn comes."

The Adventurers crowded outside the room muttered but took off, leaving to get things sorted and allowing Daniel to get to work. It was only as he finished cleaning off the bandage and applied a simple poultice to stop infection that something the Lady Marshall said struck him.

"Wait. Why aren't we using the healing station if there is one?" Daniel wondered out loud.

***

Eyes tracking over the cabinet that was the "healing station" in the room later that evening, Daniel snorted and answered his own question. It was obvious that their "healing station" was no more than a closet filled with healing potions and poultices, common healing herbs and alchemical concoctions, bandages and other forms of first aid equipment. It was all under lock and key, access blocked off via a simple enchantment available via the reception or vice-guildmasters.

Unlike smaller cities, Warmount had two vice-guildmasters to run the Guild. It was necessary due to the higher number of guild members and the time taken by the guildmaster in handling political issues. In fact, the vast majority of the guildmaster's time in the capital was spent dealing with politics, rather than the issues at the Guild. In that sense, most of the time, Adventurers would only meet the vice-guildmasters.

"I can't be the only healer in this Guild, can I?" Daniel said, looking over the healing station once more. He could not imagine how any self-respecting healer could look at what was in here and not want to overhaul the entire thing. He could spot half a dozen herbs that were well past their peak effectiveness, and at least two of the potions looked to have been handed over while devolving into their inferior quality. Never mind the lack of splints, a variety of bandages, needles, and leeches. He didn't expect them to have things like maggots inside, since that was a frontier remedy, but leeches were a timeworn and effective solution for certain kinds of poisons. Of course, you needed to know when to use and it generally was only effective against a small range of poisons—many of which were contact-based ones and not what your average Adventurer would be expected to face.

"You are not. We have two other Healers in this Guild, one a Master Healer, a second a priest of QuanEr," Lady Marshall answered Daniel. He jumped, not having heard her sneak up on him, spinning about and offering her the bow even as she continued. "The Master Healer is unfortunately too busy to manage such low-level issues, and the priest . . . the priest does not have much in terms of mundane healing skills. It is not something that he ever studied."

Daniel frowned. He knew that priests received a very different path to progress, their skills being entirely faith-based. Still, he was rather disappointed to hear that they did not even bother to study the basics of healing. What did they do when someone received a bleeding but non-life-threatening injury? Waste Mana?

"Most Adventurers learn a little first aid themselves," Lady Marshall said, almost as if she was reading his mind. "It makes surviving much easier." Daniel nodded slowly, but was apprised when she continued. "I will add it to your tasks as payment for your Guild deals, to ensure that we are properly stocked. In addition, so that matters do not devolve further, I will also arrange for you to begin giving basic first aid lessons to our members."

Dan was nodding along, happy to do the first. At the second, he blanched and opened his mouth to begin protesting. He was not, in any way, shape or form, a Master Healer. He did not feel that he was appropriately skilled to begin such lessons.

"Now get along. We've got a guildmaster to see."

Without waiting for Daniel to answer her, the Lady Marshall walked off. Leaving the healer no choice but to hurry off after her, as they ascended the stairs to the guildmaster's office.

Chapter 10

The guildmaster was a tall, languid man that the pair found lying on his couch, legs up on the edge of the couch as he propped his head up under his arm. He was dressed in the latest set of tunic and breeches that was all the rage in the capital, a series of lace collars around neck and arms. His breeches were extremely tight, so much so that Daniel could see the outline of the guildmaster's thigh muscles and the rather large item between his legs. Not that Daniel normally looked, but the use of purposeful codpieces as the new style among nobles had caused Adventurers to comment on the matter more than once. A few—a very few—Adventurers had begun to take on the court fashion, though that number even among the Adventuring nobles was low due to the vagaries of actual combat. A time and place for everything, after all.

"Adventurer Chai. For an Advanced Adventurer, you really do cause me quite a few headaches," the guildmaster said, never moving himself from the couch as Daniel was escorted in.

Lady Marshall glared at the guildmaster as he continued to laze on the couch, before she turned to leave. Only to be stopped by the guildmaster's voice.

"Stay, Carmine. Your understanding of politics might be needed."

"Guildmaster Ronson, I've asked you to use my title before." Lady Marshall tilted her head up, but contrary to her formal words, she strode across the room and helped herself to the bottle of whisky by the side, acting as though it was her own room.

"Guildmaster," Daniel said, in belated greeting.

"Could you not have kept your Gift a little quieter?" Ronson complained, turning brilliant blue eyes to fix on Daniel. Though his words were chiding, there was no hint of malice in his eyes. Just weariness.

"I . . . my apologies, Guildmaster."

"Yes, yes. Still, your charity speaks well about your character." Ronson held up his other hand, raising a finger as he continued. "As has your arrival in bolstering our recruitment numbers."

"Already?" Lady Marshall said, raising an eyebrow.

"I thought you were supposed to be keeping track of those things, my dear." Ronson smirked, but continued before she could continue. "Javier already reported the increased numbers to me. At first, he thought it was the usual variance, but the numbers keep streaming in. A Gifted Healer, even if not on their team, is a powerful draw.

"And that's nothing compared to the questions and requests to join his team. Of course, we're obligated to Adventurer Chai to make the decisions, per our agreement, but he can surely add another one or two. No?"

Daniel stayed silent, watching the pair talk, uncertain of his place in this conversation. It certainly did not seem like they were talking to him.

"No?" Ronson called out.

"Sir?" Daniel blinked. "Umm . . . maybe. It'd depend—"

"On fit. Yes, yes. And, of course, having not one but two Beastkin has put them off. You cannot imagine the kind of conversations I'm having about that."

"I think I can, sir," Daniel muttered.

"Perhaps you can." Ronson shook his head. "I will say, if you do decide to drop off one or two of them . . ."

"I won't."

"Of course not." Ronson let out a tired, weary sigh. "Then it will be as it will."

"How much longer, do you think?" Lady Marshall called out, making Ronson turn to her.

He stroked his chin with his hand then sighed again. "Another week perhaps, before we have our trials. Though *they* might want to speak with him before that."

"Yes . . ."

Silence between the pair that spoke of conversations being finished in the way old companions could. Daniel, uncertain of what they had spoken of did have a guess. "They, sir? Ma'am?"

"The royal family. The ones who called for you, of course."

"And will they—will they insist on me joining them?" Daniel said haltingly. He was uncertain if he should also add the other question, the one asking if they would back him up. But he need not have bothered, for it lay hanging between them.

"Unlikely. I" —Lady Marshall cleared her throat a little, just before she sipped on her glass of whisky— "we have an idea of what they might want."

"And that is . . . ?"

"Best left unsaid in case we're wrong," Ronson said.

Daniel made a face, but gave up when the pair refused to expand. Instead, he turned to look between the pair, curious why he had been brought forth. Nothing that had been said could not have been relayed to him.

"He's a quiet one, isn't he?" Ronson said.

"Strong too. A decent Adventurer, even with his advantages. Steady rise in the ranks. Not exceptional, but safe and steady. Hasn't lost a single party member," Lady Marshall said.

"Yes. I noted that. Makes him almost exceptional."

"Almost."

Daniel frowned more, before the pair turned to stare at him. He kept his face neutral, still wondering what they wanted.

"What you'll be facing, it will be different. You might be asked to visit noble parties, speak to royalty. Think of it like entering a new Dungeon. Learn everything you can and prepare beforehand," Ronson said, his voice dropping as he continued. "The Lady Marshall will arrange for what etiquette lessons we can fit in."

"I—"

"Will say thank you. And don't go around visiting any of your hospices. I want you learning or delving," Ronson said, holding a finger up and pointing at the healer. "That's all. Understood?"

Daniel frowned, shaking his head. "I don't understand why I can't do my usual rounds."

"Because right now, your Gift and your healing ability is leverage I can use for the Guild. If you give it away for free, especially to peasants, that leverage is going to disappear." Ronson saw the set in Daniel's lips, the narrowing in his eyes, and he sighed. "It's not forever. Just a week or two. I promise."

For a moment, the healer wavered before he nodded. Joining a Guild and receiving its protection came with certain obligations. Listening to the guildmaster was obviously one of them. In short order, he was dismissed, sent off to rest and reminded tomorrow, he'd be starting his lessons in elocution.

***

To Daniel's surprise, his teacher for the next day's lesson in elocution and etiquette was not some nobleman or lady-in-waiting but an older man with the bearing of a guard. He stood waiting for Daniel in the small room set aside for them, gesturing for Daniel to take a drink and seat, all the while watching him like a hawk. Only when Daniel had sat down did he speak.

"You might be wondering, why an old guard, eh?" At Daniel's nod, he grinned. "That's 'cause I was a Royal Guard, for all of my years, till I finished my second twenty. Now I got to find something to do, and me children don't want me in the house. So I teach Adventurers."

Daniel nodded slowly. It made sense, he guessed. Guards had to watch everything while they were on duty and, obviously, received some training as well in etiquette. A guard that paid attention probably picked up quite a bit, though discretion meant they probably could not speak of most of it. Still, general lessons in etiquette were unlikely to be barred.

"Good. You're a smart one. But Healers mostly are," the guard said. "Before you ask, you can call me Vylar."

"I'm—"

"Daniel Chai. I know. Now, here's a few things you need to understand," Vylar said. "Firstly, you and I, we're not noblemen. So what you learn isn't going to be the same. There're different ways of address. It's good to know what they are—there's a lot of little battles and details going on about which forms of address, what kinds of bows you do, that kind of thing— but we don't have the time for all that. So I'll teach you what you need to do, what you should be receiving in terms of greetings, which is nearly all the same in the context you are in, and what you should do. That's all. Got it?"

Daniel nodded.

"Good. Also, because you are an Adventurer and a healer, they'll give you a little leeway. A little only, mind you. So mind your manners and what you say," Vylar said.

"Of course."

"Har! You Adventurers always say that. Then you realize what it really means." Daniel's lips thinned, but Vylar just kept right on speaking. "Well, let's see how you do. Now, here's what you did wrong."

"Wrong?"

"When you came in, of course." Vylar sniffed. "Let's begin . . ."

Mentally groaning, Daniel stood up as Vylar waved him over to the door to take his place. Suddenly, the idea of these etiquette lessons, especially if it meant worrying about how he even entered a room, had become a lot less interesting and a lot more onerous.

Still, it was better than getting stabbed by a Kobold shiv.

***

"He stabbed me!" Zef snarled, removing his hand from his spear to bring his closed fist down on the head of the tiny, gnome-like creature. The small, four-foot humanoid crumpled, the remnants of the twisted corkscrew falling from his hands.

"Who told you to let it get that close?" Omrak rumbled. "And not wear armor?"

"My skill normally keeps me safe," Zef said as he kicked the body away. Placing his hands back on his spear, he threatened the group of Gnomes that were attempting to close on them.

Omrak, on the other side of the tight corridor, was carefully jabbing with his greatsword as he replied, "But it didn't this time, did it? Skill-breaking Skills are becoming more common. You need armor."

Daniel hummed agreement to the conversation before darting in to place a hand on Zef's back and start the healing process. He had to reach out and touch the bare skin of the lizard's back, since he needed physical contact, and the light jacket that Zef wore would disrupt his spell. He could have touched Zef's tail, but he had been told off before on that. Tails, among Beastkin, were particularly important, and touching another being's tail without her permission was similar to groping a woman without her permission. It was just not done.

Once the spell had been cast, Daniel made sure to fully retreat, giving the two frontline fighters space. He stayed low, waiting for any of the Gnomes to trickle in, even as the occasional arrow shot past him to bury itself in the enemy's body. However, Charles was arcing the shots this time, being extra careful about where and when he loosed, just in case he missed. After all, firing into a melee was a good way of injuring one's friends. This was not a hard fight anyway, it certainly wasn't one that the melee combatants couldn't finish by themselves.

This time around, the team had appeared in one of the mapped-out sections. Which meant that making their way through the first few turns was simple enough. They were only in the first few levels of the Labyrinth at this time, though they had hoped to make it deeper this time. Maybe even halfway through the maze itself. Occasionally, flashes of great ambition tried to push their way through Daniel's studied practicality, but he squashed it. The chance of them finishing an Advanced Dungeon so soon after arriving was extremely low. Even if they had completed their own, each Dungeon was different, and it behooved the Adventurers to take it seriously.

Of course, part of the reason why he wanted to progress was what the guildmaster and the vice-guildmaster had said. Almost as if he was a disappointment, with his slow and steady progress. Slow, that is, for someone with his Gifts. Yet Daniel was unwilling to pay the true Price to push his team forward. Because the faster you went, the more chance of people dying.

As Zef finally finished off the last Gnome, Daniel focused on the battle, staring at the Mana stones that littered the floor. He moved forward, helping the team pick them up before handing the stones to Asin to keep as usual, before the Catkin scampered off. Whatever the pair of Beastkin had done the day before, they had not discussed, though some of the enthusiasm that both the Kin had shown for coming to the capital had disappeared. It seemed the reality of a species hub of civilization had ground away that naïveté.

Still, none of that stopped Asin from doing her job. She scouted ahead of the team, though she was careful to not go too far. They had been warned that the Labyrinth could, at times, change even while Adventurers were inside. Walls sliding shut, others opening, and portions of the floor tilting to split parties. Of course, all of that was more common deeper inside the Labyrinth, but there was no point in taking chances.

Overall, Daniel had to acknowledge, they were doing good time. And, judging by the number of minor stones they had acquired already, the Dungeon paid decently. Of course, the capital was also more expensive, but it was no real wonder that so many adventuring teams chose to come here. Now if only Daniel could focus on adventuring and delving through the Dungeons, rather than be dragged into the politics of the country.

Chapter 11

It amazed Daniel, a little, how fast time flew by. In a blink of an eye, five days had passed, his schedule alternating between long, boring lessons on etiquette and time spent delving the Dungeon. In between, when he had Mana, Daniel ran an impromptu clinic, healing the guild members of their injuries and the occasional friend of the Guild that the Guildmaster brought along as a favor. He would have complained, considering they were still refusing to let him help at the hospices, but it had only been five days and two guests.

Still, when Zef showed up on the sixth day, just as they were supposed to enter the Dungeon, limping with one of his arms broken, Daniel was shocked. He rushed over, only for Zef to hold his hand up to forestall the healer.

"I need to inform you that I will be withdrawing from the party from today onwards," Zef said.

"What? Why?" Daniel said, his words echoed by the majority of the team. The only ones who kept quiet were Charles and Asin. The Catkin was just waiting until the others had fallen silent before she spoke to Zef in the Beastkin tongue, leaving the rest puzzled.

Zef listened for a bit, then nodded and replied quickly in the same language. Daniel leaned forward, attempting to parse the conversation. He was still struggling to learn the language and only caught a few words here and there, something about visits, payments, and fights. Between the injuries and Zef's sudden change of mind, Daniel put together the issue quickly enough.

"No!" Daniel said. "I'm not going to let you quit on us, just because someone wants to join our party."

Zef hissed a little, his tail going utterly still. He turned slitted pupils on Daniel, ire showing throughout his body and stance. "Oh, so you're going to tell me how to live my life too."

"That's not what I mean, and you know that," Daniel said.

"Do I?" Zef lifted his broken arm, still stuck in a sling. "Are you going to take my meetings for me then? Pay me back the thousand gold that they've given me to step away? You going to protect me when they insister further?"

"A thousand gold!" Daniel almost shouted.

"I might choose to leave for a thousand gold," Omrak rumbled, mostly joking. A thousand gold was a significant sum of money, enough for them to buy multiple pieces of enchanted equipment. Enough to outfit a low-Level team with basic enchanted weaponry or armor.

"Now, there, you see. With that kind of gold, I can put together my own team. Run it the way I think it should be run. Lead it myself." Zef crossed his arms, muscles bunching as he spoke. "This team has been a good opportunity, but it's not worth a thousand gold."

Daniel could not help, but still, he was reluctant to see Zef leave, especially as it would open up a space for another, unknown individual to join the team.

"You know, it's hard to progress without a healer," Daniel said.

Zef grinned, sharp, carnivorous teeth flashing in the light. Daniel was surprised to note that there were quite a few of them that were missing on one side of Zef's face. However, the Adventurer didn't seem to worry about it, and Daniel knew that was because he would regrow his teeth. One of the advantages of being a Lizardkin. Small advantages like that were common among the Beastkin compared to humans and were often used as an excuse to decry their alienness. Daniel just thought the complainers were jealous.

"I'm not too lazy to grow a team from the start. With this much funds, finding a healer at the beginning stages would be simple."

Asin, by the side, was nodding little, before she spoke up, cutting off Daniel. "Beastkin Healers. Willing to risk much."

Daniel nodded slowly, understanding coming in trickles. Beastkin Healers were in general more skilled than their counterparts, Daniel felt, since they had to deal with a much wider variety of bodies and illnesses. However, that higher requirement of knowledge also slowed down their leveling, along with the lack of resources given to them. So while there were, generally, more Beastkin Healers as a percentage of their population, there were fewer high-level ones. After all, a certain point, leveling required significant resources as a Healer, and not just the repetition of the same old acts. New, novel diseases, important personages, and new healing techniques were all requirements to level both the healing skill and their Class.

Finding a new Healer willing to risk themselves in the Dungeon among the Beastkin would be easier for Zef since additional funds could help said Healer progress, especially if they had stopped progressing already. In addition, it was all too common for Beastkin parties to work by themselves, due to the speciesism that they faced. Building up the party from the ground up, Beastkin only or not, would be the most sensible option for Zef, and even if they never made it to an Advanced Class, would still make the party a powerful and significant benefit to their communities and clans.

"And are you leaving?" Daniel could not help but ask Asin.

"No," she said, crossing her arms before her.

Zef stared at the Catkin, who returned the stare unflinchingly. Some unspoken communication passed between them before the Lizardkin snorted, turning away from the group. Daniel hesitated before reaching out. "I can still heal you . . ."

"Forget it. It'll be a good tester for my new team Healer," Zef said.

Daniel nodded and watched as the Lizardkin walked away. He sighed, turning his head around to stare at the rest of the group. "Did any of you get the offer to leave?"

To his surprise, nearly everyone except for Charles had been made an offer. When Daniel looked at Charles, the bodyguard shrugged.

"I go where the lady goes," Charles said. Now Daniel nodded. There was no need to bribe him, if one could bribe the Lady Nyssa. When he looked at her, she smiled a little and shook her head, refusing to inform him how much they had offered her. In fact, none of his other friends wanted to expand upon their bribes except for Omrak, who muttered about only being offered fifty gold.

Clapping his hand on his friend's shoulder, he dragged the big Northerner along to the Dungeon entrance. "It's okay. I'm sure they'll come and offer you something more." Watching his friend's grin bloom, Daniel could not help but add, "Just don't take it, right."

The reminder made Omrak sad, but he did not protest, leaving the team to cross into the Dungeon, one party member less.

***

Seventeen turns later, the team were caught in another desperate battle. Without Zef to hold the frontline along with Omrak, Daniel had taken his place alongside his friend once more. Unfortunately, unlike Zef, Daniel did not have the dedicated volume of Skill Proficiencies dedicated to damage, decreasing the number of monsters that he killed. In general, this was not a major issue, though it did slow their progress down. In fact, they had intended to turn around at the very next bend before they had been ambushed.

The team were caught up in a desperate battle against the Stone Golems that faced them, creatures who were shaped as a variety of monsters that the team had faced. Each Golem was slow in its attacks, but supernaturally strong and immune to the majority of penetrating and cutting attacks. Of course, Omrak's own skill made his weapon incredibly durable, allowing him to whale upon the Golems without concern for damage. And Daniel's hammer was immensely suited to this task, shattering stone limbs and heads.

Unfortunately, people like Charles and Asin were forced to use their Skill Proficiencies again and again to penetrate the tough stone armor. Both fighters were panting, their Skills using both Mana and stamina to imbue their attacks, whether it was **Penetration** by Asin or **Drilling Arrow** by Charles. That they were trapped by another pair of elementals that had emerged from the ground and put the entire party at even greater risk meant they had to go all out and were unable to support the two front liners.

The most powerful member of the group, Lady Nyssa, had taken it upon herself to do the most damage, throwing **Sonic Orbs** down the corridor, cracking stone by its very vibrations. Unfortunately, the loud shrieks also damaged her party members, even through the enchantments they wore. After all, to crack the stone creatures she had to crank up the power of her attacks, leaving all of them reeling.

In desperation, the team kept on hammering away at the Stone Golems, even as their circle of protection shrunk with each passing second.

Daniel ducked another punch, swinging his hammer to crack the arm. But an unseen punch came in from his side, hitting his shield arm and forcing him to stagger backwards. He bumped into Asin, throwing her off and getting her clipped with a strike too, forcing the Catkin to sprawl to the ground. Even as the pair tried to recover their tempo, Omrak fell back, loosing a roar of rage as he triggered **Thundering Strike** to shatter the creature facing him, giving him space to aid the pair.

Lady Nyssa, in the center of their shrunken formation, was sucking down a Mana potion, refilling her empty pool. Almost immediately, the magical concoction helped push her energy higher, though she held off casting, knowing that they might have to risk a powerful final attack by her.

"Well, this is concerning. Do you need help?" a voice called, alerting the group.

Daniel was surprised to notice the quartet before them. They were a strange group, for three of them wore powerful, highly enchanted plate mail and wielded paired swords and shields in the same griffin motif. A part of Daniel's mind struggled to place the motif, knowing that he had seen it before. Mostly though, his attention was drawn to the grinning, and entirely relaxed, blond boy at the head of the team.

That level of relaxation was surprising to Daniel, since the Dungeon was not a place to be relaxed at all. This was the kind of behavior that saw individuals dead, no matter how powerful their protectors.

"Yes!" Omrak shouted, smashing the pommel of his sword into a gripping arm. He had to hit it three times, suffering blows from another five-foot high, lizard-like Golem in the side before he managed to free himself. "There is no dishonor in asking for aid when one needs it. And we need it!"

"Oh, very well, then. Sir Marmonth," the young boy said. One of the guards, Sir Marmonth, Daniel assumed, noted and gestured with his fingers to two of his friends. The next moment, the pair of Adventurers flickered, crossing the distance of the hallway in seconds.

It would take Daniel time to piece together exactly what happened in the next few seconds. The guards had moved with such speed and precision that they had chopped apart, crushed, and destroyed the various Golems among the team, and returned to their starting positions, never once having disturbed the party themselves. In a few short breaths, Daniel and his friends were left standing in a cloud of settling dust and falling rock.

"That seems to be that. Good luck!" the teenager called and resumed walking, heading through them and most likely, out of the Dungeon too. Daniel was still trying to piece things together when he felt a hand pulling on his sleeve. It was quite insistent, forcing Daniel to bow and step aside to allow the quartet to pass.

Daniel turned his head, wanting to ask only to find Lady Nyssa glaring at him, one knee bent. In fact, Daniel realized, his entire team were bowing.

It was only as they were passing, that Daniel realized who they were. It should have been obvious to him; if not for the low Mana and the desperation of the moment, he would have known. After all, the manticore was the shield design of the royal family. And the boy, while Daniel might never have seen him, was exactly the right age for the third prince.

It was as they were slowly making their way out that Charles had to remark, "Well, that happened."

And, Daniel had to admit, it was as good a summary of the day as anything.

***

Even after all this time, the royal family had yet to make time to see Daniel. It was frustrating, if not for the fact that his days were packed with lessons on etiquette and delving. Eight days had passed since his talk with the guildmaster and finally, the Guild had informed him that they were ready to start the interviews for replacements to his party. The two replacements that he had to fill now.

In the meantime, Daniel had heard about the increased pressure his friends had faced to leave. Omrak had even grown quiet about how much he was being offered, while Asin rarely left the guildhall unless she was in the company of others. When Daniel had asked why, she had muttered something about matted fur and refused to expand further.

Lady Nyssa had been the least bothered it seemed with the entire issue, though she had taken to spending less time with the team as a whole. When pressed, she had muttered something about family and social obligations before changing the topic. With his recent lessons, Daniel could not help but sympathize a little more with her.

For the first time since they had arrived, outside of delving, the entire team was together. They had been provided one of the larger drawing rooms and the Guild had even provided refreshments, which Omrak was now busy devouring. Inside, the vice-guildmaster was looking around, the Lady Marshall waving Daniel over as he debated which seat to take in the opposed seating arrangement of couches that had been set up.

"Do you normally do all this?" Daniel said, knowing that the interviewees were all placed in a separate drawing room with even more refreshments within.

"Of course not. Most just get the smaller drawing room, if they even bother to ask," Lady Marshall said. "But you're our healer. And considering the class of people coming by, it's to our advantage to put our best foot forward."

"And mmmphhfff . . . good food it is!" Omrak said, around a stuffed mouth.

"She said foot, not food," Daniel corrected.

The teenage Northerner just waved a fried breadstick at Daniel dismissively, to which the healer could only roll his eyes. His own stomach was tight with worry, driving away all appetite. In fact, he had twisted knots in his guts, making him consider using his Gift to ease his anxiety. Briefly.

"Now, I recommend you be in the middle. It is you they will be listening to and wanting to meet," Lady Marshall was saying and Daniel forced himself to focus. "Your friends should not speak, especially Asin."

"Why her?" Daniel frowned.

"Because she is a Beastkin and some of the nobles will be unhappy about that as it is," Lady Marshall said.

"That sounds like a good reason for Asin to speak up more then," Daniel said.

The aforementioned Catkin turned from where she was busy dipping thin slices of fried meat into a red sauce that made Daniel's nose water even from the few feet that separated them. She shook her head quite vigorously at his suggestion, making Daniel grimace.

"Your friend has better sense than you," Lady Marshall said, only to be interrupted.

"No. No like talk," Asin clarified.

Lady Nyssa, behind, coughed into her hand, only to look placidly at Lady Marshall when the vice-guildmaster looked at her. She did, however, speak up. "I think, Daniel, that anyone who has a major issue with Asin would have left by now. And we can be certain to make it clear that Asin will not be leaving the party."

Daniel nodded reluctantly. There were some fights that just were not worth taking on.

"Good. Now, sit down. We have to begin." Lady Marshall chivied the group to sit, only Charles taking a station behind Lady Nyssa even after Daniel's request to sit. Once they were situated, Lady Marshall headed for the door, stopping to turn and glare at the group, half of whom had plates stacked with food before them. "And *try* to put on a good showing, if you can."

Warning given, she left to bring in the first scion of the noble houses. Daniel, seated in the middle of the group in a chair of his own, could not help but shake his knee, jittering with suppressed energy. Interviewing these new potential party mates was more nerve-wracking than he had expected.

The first to come in was an older man, in his late twenties to Daniel's eye. He still had the clear complexion that was so common among the nobles, but there were little lines along the eyes, a little maturity to his face that those still coming out of their teens had yet to achieve. He strode in, nodding absently to the vice-guildmaster who had held the door open and showed him the way before she murmured to one of the servants who would be taking over her work, and took the seat positioned for him.

"I am Lord Taylor Zaynastra." He touched the sword by his hip, a thinner, longer weapon than what was normally wielded by Adventurers. "I am a Level 29 Duelist."

"Duelist?" Daniel said, frowning.

"It's a combat class. Mostly focused on individual fights against a single opponent, though Lord Zaynastra has significant experience dueling multiple opponents. He is also a Master of the sword, even though he has not mentioned that," Lady Nyssa said, offering the other lord a quick smile. "I hope that's not too presumptuous, m'lord."

"Not at all."

Omrak cocked his head to the side, eyeing the nobleman before he spoke. "What Adventurer rank are you?"

"I have none," Lord Zaynastra.

"Then what are you doing here?" Daniel blurted out.

"I will receive a pass from the Beginner Classes due to my Levels."

When Daniel looked over at Lady Nyssa, she lowered her voice to whisper, the other lord having paused to allow her to make the explanation. "Combat Classers of significant skill can receive waivers to enter Advanced

Dungeons if they have sufficient Levels and have passed a test."

"Right. I guess that's good," Daniel said, already feeling frustrated. This was not going the way he thought matters would go. On the other hand, at least he was not feeling scared or tense anymore. "But why do you want to go Adventuring now?"

"I do not." Seeing that his words had startled the group, he clarified. "The royal family considers Adventuring a necessity among the nobles. Reaching a Master Level will open additional opportunities for myself and my family." He nodded to Daniel. "You will help ensure I do so in the fastest and safest method."

"Oh, right." Daniel glanced at his friends, curious if any of them had further questions. They all shook their heads, before Daniel turned to the Duelist. He was already standing, nodding to the group.

"Good. I expect to hear from you by the end of the day."

And before they could correct him, he had left. Daniel had to admit, if nothing else, the

Duelist had placed a significant amount of points into his Agility, the way he could move.

"I guess, next?" Daniel said. When a head popped in, the attendant charged with dealing with the other interviewees checking on them, he repeated the last word again. This time, more firmly.

***

"I'm . . . I'm . . . an Advanced Adventurer." The young man breathed, looking visibly nervous. He looked up to the side where his mother was standing, glaring at him and gulped. He turned back to Daniel, continuing, "I got it last year. I'm at Level ummm . . ."

"Johan!" his mother barked.

"Right, uhh, sorry. Sorry, I'm not supposed to . . . ummm . . . say." Johan bobbed his head low. "But I've got Inventory."

"What weapon do you use?" Daniel said, glancing at the short sword Johan wore at his side. "That?"

"Uhh, I'm a Master of Arms," Johan said. "After Inventory, I switched back to Master of Arms."

Daniel could not help but let out a low whistle. Even he had heard of the Class. It was an extremely tough Class to acquire since it required mastery of multiple weapons. Those who received it were often older Adventurers or trainers or prodigies.

"Team?" Asin said, speaking up.

The pair of nobles seated opposite of them both looked at Asin. However, instead of the usual sneering disgust at her nature, one was nervous and the other considering.

"I, well, I joined a few ummm . . . noble teams. You know the kind."

"We don't," Omrak said.

"Nobles don't always join the Guilds. It adds another level of politics, so for the younger crowd, they often work together to form teams. They can be permanent to semi-permanent to random . . ." Lady Nyssa explained. "Though, at the Advanced stage, most will choose to join a

Guild. The advantages start outweighing the ease of teams and, of course, the dangers increase."

"Right. She's right. The Lady Nyssa, that is." Johan flushed again. "But, you know, that's why I'm here." He offered a tight smile, then ducked his head.

"Of course. And that's good of you to be here," Daniel said, then looked at the stern mother. "Both of you."

He only got a *hmpphf* in response, so he turned away. Best focus on the interview.

***

"I'm a Battle Alchemist," the young woman before them said, her body smelling of potions and herbs. Asin had backed off the moment she had entered the room and was now standing at the farthest corner of the room next to an open window, her tail lashing out behind her. "I have a few healing globes . . ." The fair-haired brunette hefted a couple of swirling red globes. "But I mostly focus on damage and debuffs."

"Globes?" Daniel said, holding a hand out. The young lady happily handed it to him, her eyes glowing. "This is not glass."

"It's something my Master came up with. Rather than using potions, we use these. The material breaks when we need it to but is otherwise quite tough," Reeves said. "You throw it at your target, and the liquid seeps into them."

"How about armor?" Daniel asked.

"Well . . . that's one of the problems," Reeves said, sighing. "I need more materials, more money to work out the way to do it. Right now, the potion is partially injected through Mana transference, but it's only a little better than a tenth. Otherwise, you need direct skin-to-liquid contact."

"And your other globes are like that?" Lady Nyssa said, eyeing the half-dozen small orbs all across the woman's body. It was surprising to see her, since the last half-dozen applicants had been nobles. It seemed that some candidates were just that good that the guildmaster had wanted them to interview no matter what.

"Yes. Air-based poisons and debuffs work well, and the explosive ones are a non-issue. I was experimenting with a dual-globed one, with an explosive outer layer first and the secondary potion beneath to expose the body beneath with my last party before . . ."

"Before?" An arched eyebrow from Lady Nyssa.

"I fixed the problem! It won't explode anymore," Reeves said, her eyes wide as she realized her mistake. "Now, you have to inject a little Mana before the globes begin their breakdown. It's all good."

Lady Nyssa made a little noise in her throat, her doubt quite clear. Daniel, on the other hand, smiled a little before speaking up.

"So why this team? Alchemists of all kinds are always in demand with Guilds."

Reeves gave Daniel a look of disbelief, as if she could not understand how he could ask that question. "Because you're a Gifted Healer, of course. I don't want to die before I perfect these."

Asin, by the windows, let out a snort, and Omrak burst out laughing, clapping Daniel on the shoulder as he flushed at the obvious answer.

Of course they wanted him for his healing.

They all did.

***

"I'm a Level 18 Nobleman," Lord Biber stated imperiously.

"And what does that do?" Daniel asked.

"I have Class Skills that increase the yields of my holdings, map out and regenerate my mines, increase the health and population fertility . . ."

Daniel held a hand up, cutting Lord Biber short. Nine interviews in, and he was growing tired of the way these nobles could just go on and on if he let them. "I meant, what does it do in the Dungeon?"

"Nothing. Why would I take Skill Proficiencies that are so wasteful?" Lord Biber said, looking puzzled.

"Right." Daniel nodded. "Next!"

***

The young noblewoman before him was dressed more for a court dance than an Adventurers interview. A very non-energetic court dance, since she was threatening to spill out with every breath she took. Every deep breath, as she leaned forwards and answered Daniel's questions.

"And I do think you should visit me and my sisters at our home, I'm sure we could find some way to . . . *entertain you,*" Lady Harrington said, breathing out gently, curled red hair bobbing artfully around her heart-shaped face.

"Yes . . ." Daniel said, then shook his head. He pushed against the subtle Skill she was using, the Charisma, and focused on the mindset he kept while working on patients. "But your Skills don't really seem suitable for the Dungeon."

"No, I guess not. A pity. But my mother always said there are better Skills for a noblewoman." A cutting glance at the seated noblewoman beside Daniel, before she rose, smiling. "Another time, then."

"Yes, of course."

"I think we should take her . . ." Omrak said, eyes trailing after the noblewoman as she sashayed out of the room, the door closing after her.

"Men!" Lady Nyssa muttered, while beside them, back in her seat with her legs up on the chair, Asin chuffed in agreement.

Daniel and Charles were smart enough to not reply.

***

"Level 21 Knight, an Advanced Class for two years. I expect to make it to Master Class in another three," Lord Julian, the muscular nobleman before them, said. "I believe your team, with my aid, will be able to achieve similar results."

"That's . . . good," Daniel said hesitantly.

Over by his side, Daniel could not help but notice that Lady Nyssa was sitting up a lot straighter and smiling demurely at the knight.

"I'm sure you could . . ." Lady Nyssa said breathily.

"Do you require your mount?" Charles said, speaking up for the first time during the day. "Most Knights focus their specializations on mounted combat."

"I have a few that benefit from that," Lord Julian said, running a hand through his hair idly. Doing so made his bulging arm muscles stand out in stark relief to his tight shirt sleeves for a second. "But I have also trained in traditional sword-and-shield combat when unmounted."

"That breastplate, it's enchanted?" Daniel said, feeling the slight thrum in energy from even his seat. Which meant that it was likely highly enchanted.

"Yes. My entire suit of plate mail is. Minor enchantments only, in durability, toughness, lightness and magical absorption. A major enchantment in stored kinetic reflection."

"A powerful piece of enchantment then. It's all linked?" Lady Nyssa said, eyes gleaming with interest. At Lord Julian's nod, she smiled. "That must be quite expensive to keep running."

"My family can handle it."

"Of course, of course," Lady Nyssa said, appreciatively.

By the side, Omrak rolled his eyes a little when he met Daniel's gaze. Still, they both glanced at Lord Julian's sword, whose hilt was simple and practical, much like the breastplate. Minimal designs, showing a man who actually used his equipment.

***

Man after man, woman after woman, the group listened to the applicants. It was late afternoon, after a single, all-too-short break for lunch, that the constant stream of individuals had an interruption. Instead of the usual nobleman shown in by the attendant, a pair of guards entered first, scanning the room. Only when they were sufficiently satisfied that no dangers lurked within did the next applicant enter.

By this point, the entire group were on their feet, bowing. How could they not be? The tabard on the guards were a clear indicator of who they were to speak with next. And if they did not remember the griffin, the fact that they had seen these very guards a bare few days ago was reminder enough.

"Your highness. You honor us," Lady Nyssa said, leading the group as they all quickly echoed her sentiments.

"Please. Don't." The young boy took a seat, gesturing for them to sit down too. When they hesitated, he glared at the group and the guards standing beside him, the last one having taken station outside the now closed door, stared at the team till they reluctantly sat too. "I want you to interview me just like any other member of your potential team."

Daniel shared a glance with the others, his heart having started racing at the mention of the interview. Lady Nyssa shook her head a little while Asin, beside the group, was eyeing the guards more than the prince. Omrak coughed, trying not to laugh directly in the prince's face.

"Is there something wrong, Hero Omrak, son of Losin?" the prince said.

"Dry throat, your highness," Omrak said, pounding his chest.

"Please, stop. Just call me Roland," Prince Roland said.

"Hero—"

"Your highness, please. This is not appropriate," Lady Nyssa cut in, glaring at Omrak who looked at her puzzled. "We could be punished if we are found to use your name inappropriately."

Prince Roland frowned, then turned sideways to one of his guards. He spoke up, his voice growing magisterial. "Please note this down and ensure all the royal guards, Daniel Chai, Lady Nyssa, and the remainder of their team have been provided the right to call me by first name without honorifics. No punishment or other form of retribution will be placed upon them, upon pain of breaching Royal Command."

The guard bowed, his face entirely calm and expressionless. Still, Daniel felt there was a little bit of a long-suffering resignation in the man's eyes.

"Now, see. All taken care of. Call me Roland, or I'll be upset," Prince Roland said.

"Of course . . . Roland." Lady Nyssa bowed.

"Troublesome," Omrak rumbled, glaring at Lady Nyssa. "He asked—we should have just done it."

"See! How easy is that?" Prince Roland said.

"Easy for a . . . Northerner," Charles muttered. It was obvious to Daniel he had meant to use another word, but chosen to switch it at the end. Daniel frowned a little, surprised to hear the degree of animosity. Then again, Charles had always been stuck up about such things, only willing to bend a little because they were all Adventurers. Faced with actual royalty . . .

"Now, how do we do this?" Roland said, rubbing his hands together in elation. He looked quite excited, eager for them to interview him.

"Ummm," Daniel said, realizing the rest of the team were silent. "We generally get an introduction from the applicant. Name, Class, that kind of thing. Of course, with you . . ."

"No, no. We should do this right," Roland said with a firm nod. "I'm Prince Roland

Nimbler, fourth in line to the throne after my brothers and sister. I am a Level 11 Royal Prince, with Skills in personal combat and team combat." He paused, considering, and touched his sword. "I also have a full complement of enchanted equipment, though they are all only Masterwork quality."

"Only?" Omrak choked.

"Yes. I told my mother that I would only take Masterwork," Prince Roland said, his eyes gleaming with fervor. "I didn't want to have too much of an advantage."

Daniel coughed into his hand, forcibly making himself look down and stare at the glass of water he was picking up as he tried not to visibly scoff at the prince. He had no idea what an advantage he already had, did he?

"Will your guards be joining us as well, Roland?" Lady Nyssa said, eyeing the three Griffin Guards.

"Oh, no! That's why I'm interviewing. You'll all be my party," Roland said, excitedly. "They were just with me because I had trouble finding a proper party."

"Why us?" Asin asked, her tail having stopped its slow thrashing around and was now almost directly rigid behind her.

"Why, Daniel of course. My parents said the only way I would be allowed to have a proper team, it had to be with him," Prince Roland said, nodding firmly. "So I do hope you take me."

Daniel looked at his team, trying to understand how any of this was a request. After all, this was the prince they were talking to, someone in the line of succession to rule their nation. If the guildmaster had an inkling of this—as did the rest of the nobles—it would explain the large lineup they had faced. Still, Daniel forced a smile onto his face, strained as it was.

"Of course . . . Roland. We'll just have to . . . finish the interview."

Chapter 12

The day was finally over, and the group slumped in various positions throughout the room. Daniel, in particular, was looking exhausted, having taken over the entire couch as he lay there, a hand over his eyes. Lady Nyssa had moved over to the interview chair in the meantime while Asin stalked the floor, passing before the windows as the waning sun streamed in.

"That was a disaster . . ." Daniel groaned, never bothering to look up.

"Our heads are still on our necks, so I think that is arguable," Lady Nyssa said, trying for levity. It fell flat around the room, none of them feeling it.

"He seems like a good man at least," Omrak said.

"He's a prince. He doesn't have to be a good man," Charles said, speaking up. "He just needs to be a prince."

"I meant he seemed to want to be a good Adventurer," Omrak said. "Unlike some of the others we saw."

"Yes, but choosing him . . . it's complicated," Lady Nyssa said, biting her lower lip.

"No. Simple. Choose. He asked," Asin said.

"Not that simple. What if he gets hurt?" Lady Nyssa said concernedly.

"Daniel."

"And if he can't heal him?" Lady Nyssa rebutted.

Daniel let out a snort. "Then he's probably dead."

"And that's somehow supposed to comfort us?" Lady Nyssa shook her head, before she hesitantly added, "It's not just that. There are good reasons to not choose him at all."

"What good reason could that be?" Daniel said, frowning. He heard something in her voice that made him sit up and look at the noblewoman who eventually chose to speak.

"It's . . . well, there are rumors his choices aren't supported by his parents. They might be happier if we chose not to let him join us," she said.

"Will they protect us from an upset prince, then?" Omrak said. "Where I come from, we do not have princes, but we hear the stories. Of your lords who choose to act on their whims rather than rule with conscience."

"Careful . . ." Charles hissed. "'Ware how you speak, for you speak of royalty."

"And so, man must learn to watch their words rather than choose truth and honor," Omrak grumbled.

"That—"

"No, both of you," Daniel said. "This is not the time to begin this argument. We have bigger problems."

"Yes, yes you do." The voice cut through their hubbub, making the group turn. Standing before them was Guildmaster Ronson, somehow having entered the room silently.

"You knew," Daniel said accusingly.

"Of course I did. I arranged for this, in fact," Ronson said. "You would not believe the kind of security and protocol that is involved in setting up his visit. Or the kind of changes we've had to make in anticipation of you taking him on."

"You want us to hire him," Daniel said flatly.

"Yes. It'd do the Guild great good." Guildmaster Ronson smiled, rubbing his hands together a little. "And you would not believe the kind of payback I'd be able to get."

"And if he dies?"

"Don't let him," Ronson stated. When Daniel rolled his eyes, the guildmaster grew firmer. "It's not that hard. Just don't push that hard. He'll also be decked out in more enchanted equipment than your entire party." He paused, then smiled a little. "And if you play your cards right, so will all of you."

Omrak perked up at that, while Asin cocked her head to the side, eyes swiveling forward as she stopped her pacing. Lady Nyssa continued to sit there serenely, not at all surprised by the statement. Daniel got it after a second. The best way to keep their child safe was to make them strong too, after all.

In truth, Daniel was uncertain how he felt about that. Loot was good, but this was not loot that they had earned. This was given to them, just like his Gift. And just like his Gift, there would be a price to pay. What it was and whether they were willing to pay it, well . . .

Charles, of them all, was the least affected by thoughts of greed. "Are you going to inform them about the additional dangers that adding him will create?"

"Mmmm . . . I would have. But it's obvious you want to do so." Guildmaster Ronson looked less than impressed, but he stayed silent while Charles took over the floor. He even stepped a few steps forward from his usual position behind Lady Nyssa to speak.

"Adding the third prince to the party will embroil the team in capital politics. That is over and above any minor political issues that having my lady in the party has already added." Charles paused, seeing Lady Nyssa staring at him with annoyance. He sketched a small bow to her. "I'm sorry, Miss, but I have obligations to your parents as well."

"Traitor," she said, but without any true rancor.

"As I was saying, capital politics is more active and biased than what you have been exposed to already. There will be additional demands on the prince to do his duties, few as they might be, being the third prince, which will invariably include us," Charles said. He gestured at Daniel, who was listening silently. "Daniel has already begun the process of acquiring the skills necessary to pass among the nobles, but if we accept the prince, all of the party will be forced to study." He nodded to Lady Nyssa. "Even my mistress will be adding to her political studies, as the winds of change politically increase."

"I'm sorry," Omrak said, arms crossed. "But what does all that mean?"

"Ah." Charles blinked, trying to find the words to explain things simpler.

"You will be going to a lot of balls, public appearances, and other social events with nobles. Maybe even be invited to the occasional royal event, and any of your successes—or failures—will be highlighted and lauded or derided by the populace," Guildmaster Ronson said. "But that's the least of the problems you face."

"Least?" Asin asked, and Daniel noted that her tail was slowly moving, entirely stiff behind her.

"Yes. Least," Guildmaster Ronson's said. "You'll face a more perilous future, potentially even in attacks directly on you. I expect there might be additional pressure on the Beastkin population once it's clear that you're part of the party too." Asin nodded, as if already having considered part of that. "But more importantly, you'll also be targets for individuals wanting to embarrass the royal family, destroy their prestige, or even kill the third prince."

Daniel frowned, speaking up. "He's only the third prince. Why would it matter?"

"He might not be the next in succession, but he's also the one who's most vulnerable. While killing him would be less of a win, it would be one that is easier to acquire."

"And you're saying that the nobles would want to kill him?" Daniel said, looking at Charles and then Ronson. "I didn't think things were that vicious."

"Maybe a few, but more likely, enemies from abroad," Ronson said.

Unfortunately, that was something that Daniel could understand. While Brad was generally at peace with the neighboring countries, but in the obvious Orc lands to the west, the landlocked kingdom was also prone to getting caught up in the occasional battles with ambitious kingdoms on its borders.

"And you still want us to take them on," Daniel exclaimed.

"As your guildmaster. Yes," Ronson replied.

Omrak chuckled a little, before he spoke up. "I am still for it. Hero does not coil from potential dangers. And assassination is a coward's way of winning a battle."

"Well, I think you have a sufficient understanding of the dangers and our desires," Ronson said. "I won't force the issue, as promised. You have full control over who joins your team. I will add one last word of caution. Whoever you choose to join your team, for the second open slot, will see a significant increase in their social standing as well. That kind of political influence has seen significant kinds of pressure brought upon others before. Especially the commoners."

Daniel winced again, and by the time he was finished collecting his thoughts, Ronson had left the room, leaving the team to sit around once more.

"So are we making a decision or not?" Omrak said, voicing the thoughts of everyone.

***

The answer was not. They argued and talked for a little more, with Daniel staying silent. His thoughts spiraled continuously, bouncing from concern to excitement to even deeper worry. The potential liabilities of acquiring the third prince were weighed against the simple enthusiasm of the man, along with the unspoken dangers of angering a member of the royal family. When the group had to call on Daniel for the third time, they gave up on any further discussion for the time being, breaking up to tackle their own powers.

Daniel barely even noticed that, still seated on the couch. Eventually, they left him slumped down and lying on it once more, his mind refusing to grasp a single thought. Concerns over his party, about what would happen, and the potential dangers that he was exposing his friends to tightened his stomach, creating knots in his guts.

Hours Daniel lay on the couch, only interrupted once when the Lady Marshall looked in on him. She saw him lying there, staring into space, and closed the door behind her, not even letting the servants enter. In the end, by the time he was able to pull himself from his circling thoughts, the day was late.

Unwilling to continue lying there, the healer stood up abruptly. He walked right out of the Guild, turning down now familiar roads in search of a place to eat as his growling stomach demanded. His thoughts were still muddled, though all that he felt was a quiet, continuous buzz in his brain.

"Adventurer Chai." The voice startled Daniel, taking him out of his thoughts.

He looked around, realizing that somehow the normally busy alleyway that he walked through at the stop had emptied itself out. Now, there were only four thugs in front of him. Because it was quite clear, from their scruffy appearance to their leering grins, that they were thugs. Automatically, Daniel shifted his feet, going into an ablated angle towards those in front and turning his head enough so that he could look behind. Two more ruffians stood behind, hemming him in.

"That's me," Daniel said, trying to project confidence. He could summon his sword and shield easily, since he always stored them in his inventory. Armor, on the other hand, he kept in his room. Even if he had brought it, he'd still have to put it on, so that was out. Too bad he wasn't wearing much of anything else in terms of protection, never truly expecting to be caught up like this.

"Good. You know what this is, don't you?" The leader, the one in front, said. She sported a dirty blonde hair cut, one that looked like someone had taken her dagger to it while blind drunk. A small scar across his lip made it seem as though he was sneering all the time.

"A robbery?" Daniel said. "I don't carry that much gold on me. Most of it is held by the Adventurers Guild."

The leader laughed, before he shook his head. "We'll take the money, but we are mostly here to beat a lesson into you."

Daniel frowned. "What makes you think I'd give you my money then, if you're going to beat me anyway?"

"Because we can make it a lot worse." A gesture at his side made the leader's friends span out, taking up the rest of the room in front of Daniel. Shuffling feet from behind him told Daniel that the others were closing in. He shifted his position again, putting more of his back to the wall even as he stuck his hand out sideways and yanked for his shield first.

"Interesting. Most go for their weapons." The leader didn't seem at all worried, the bandits chuckling.

Daniel realized why soon after as an unseen energy tugged at his shield, just as he was beginning to slip it on fully. It surprised him, forcing him to turn his attention to keeping hold of his equipment, and leaving him exposed.

The sap came down hard, catching Daniel on an instinctively raised shoulder. It clipped the top of his ear and the top of his shoulder, sending him staggering to the side a little. The tugging on his shield increased in strength, but that jarring motion at least helped Daniel slip his hand fully through the straps.

Instinct drove his feet, letting himself roll with the blow, avoiding a follow-up attack that only caught on the edges of his back. It hurt, but the padded sap only bruised his ribs.

Shield Bash triggered as Daniel threw himself into the first of the bandits that assaulted him from behind. He crashed into his opponent backwards, throwing them a few feet away, and opening up a line. He managed all three steps, before he felt the rope tangle itself around his foot. Then they yanked on it.

He fell crashing to the ground face first, even as he was dragged backwards. Bruises formed across his arm and his chest for he had used them to cushion his fall, and now the sap and baton crashed into his back. Daniel hunched over instinctively, trying to protect his head, twisting around to bring his shield upwards for protection.

"Feisty for a healer. But they did tell me that you would be. One of the foolish ones, someone who thinks they should be on the front lines. Foolish." The leader had stayed where she was, not moving, instead taunting Daniel.

The thugs quickly clustered around him, batons and saps coming crashing down on his body. They were all slightly bad, meant to hurt and injure rather than kill. Even as Daniel fought off as many of the blows as he could with his shield, he noted that they never tried to strike his head at all, not since the first blow at least. A hint of what they wanted started to percolate through his mind, but his focus was on the battlefield before him.

Perin's Blow was Daniel's next attempt at defense. It wasn't a shield-based skill, but since **Shield Bash** was still on cooldown, this would do. Additionally, the knockback effect of the attack, even blunted by the unsuitability of the shield, meant that when he thrusted into the thigh of his opponent, it sent the thug flying into the wall, to bounce bonelessly off it as his head impacted.

For a second, Daniel rebelled in his minor victory, before another boot came in low and kicked forwards to strike an exposed floating rib. He felt it crack, pain lancing through his body, and instinctively hunched over, curling up on the ground as he tried to protect it from further damage. The foot retracted as he groaned in pain and someone snatched his shield off from him, his straps suddenly cut.

Another half dozen blows, leaving Daniel purple and bruised, before the group pulled back. Another chuckle as the assailant leader spoke. "Now, probably much more in a positive mindset to listen, aren't you?"

All Daniel could do was groan as he attempted to catch his breath.

"I thought so. So here's the message. Get rid of the Catkin and the Northerner."

Daniel frowned, his body aching but his mind a little puzzled at just a single message. An unseen gesture, and the other thugs reached over, hauling him upwards. Daniel frowned, his body in contact with at least two of his assailants. For a brief, brief moment, Daniel considered using his Gift in a different way. It would be the simplest thing in the world, to reach out and touch their blood vessels. Stop the heart, tear open the battery. He could even do something to the brainstem, if he wanted it to be faster. Then, instinctive revulsion, one born of countless hours putting his Gift, his skills, into practice doing the opposite ran through him. Part of Daniel also felt that doing so would be a betrayal, a true traitorous betrayal of the Gift that Erlis had given him.

"Now, did you hear me?" The leader was up close to Daniel's face, glaring at him.

"Yes . . . but is that it?" he said. He could not keep the surprise from his voice, as he wondered about the simple, singular requests.

"For now. Did you think we were going to tell you, give you hints, of who our employee was?" Again, that annoying smirk, that confident tone.

"No." Daniel gauged the distance and threw himself forward, trying to smash his forehead into the other's. He was jerked backwards by the pair holding him up long before he reached the other, the thugs well used to such tricks.

"And then you do that. And here I thought we had come to an understanding. I guess we'll just have to beat you a little more, until you get it properly," the thug spoke, gesturing to the others. Daniel's arms were held tight, even as he tried to free himself. He could only attempt to roll with the attacks as the other thugs laid into him.

Countless minutes passed in a blur before the thugs finally released him, allowing Daniel to lie on the ground, covered in blood and bruises of his own. At least half of his ribs were cracked, and at one point, they'd taken to punching his jaw and face, leaving his tongue bruised and bloodied.

Worse than the physical beating though, as he slowly recuperated and managed to cast a

Healer's Mark on himself to begin the healing, was the embarrassment. He was a healer and Adventurer. Supposedly stronger, more deadly than any civilian. And even if they were thugs, people who had the semi-combat Class, they were not Adventurers.

They did not fight for their life every day.

But they had taken him, beaten him like he was but a child. A civilian. That shame burned even worse than the injuries that he slowly stitched together with Mana and his Gift. The only thing that Daniel could hope for was that one day this shame would be washed away by his own Gift.

Until then, he could only hope that he'd be able to find these thugs at some point. And return the favor, with interest. Because if there was one thing that the hard-headed ex-Miner was not going to do, it was to get rid of his friends.

Chapter 13

"What happened to you?" Lady Marshall hissed as Daniel walked back into the Guild. He was carrying a roll of bread and meat in one hand, his hammer strapped to his side and shield—left behind by the thugs—strapped to his arm. He had received more than one look from the guard, but as an Adventurer, they had not stopped him.

"I got into an argument with some rather rude thugs." Daniel brushed against his clothing, all of it stained with mud and the remnants of the trashing he had received.

There were even layers of blood on it, from when the blows had torn skin and split his lip. Of course, he was uninjured due to his own healing skills but that did not stretch towards his clothing.

"Where's my team?"

"I don't know." Lady Marshall's eyes widened. "I'll send for them immediately." She turned, calling out to the hall, voice ringing through the building. It was surprising how such an elegant young woman had such a strident, penetrating voice. Within seconds, various attendants had arrived, as well as other curious guild members. Lady Marshall barked orders, insisting that they drag as many of Daniel's people to her immediately. She also sent others to check if any of them had left, before gesturing for Daniel to follow her to a nearby waiting room.

"Thank you." And he was really grateful that she was so quick on the uptake, for if they had attacked him, who knew what they might have done to his friends. In particular, he was worried about Asin. The general distaste for the Beastkin in the kingdom, and the increased speciesism in the capital, worried him. Thankfully for his heart, Asin was the first to appear, pushing open the courtyard door.

"Fight?" Asin said as she walked in. She was sniffing the air, smelling Daniel and the scents on him, as a tail swished behind her.

"Yes. Six of them." Shame rushed through Daniel again as he hung his head. "I only managed to fight one of them off. The rest . . ." He trailed off, unable to even offer any further excuse.

"No shame in losing to overwhelming force," Lady Marshall said. "And it's likely the ones they sent for you were decently leveled. It's not like you were fighting beginner monsters again." She chuckled. "Anyway, at your level, even six beginner monsters might be a bit of a push."

That last sentence rankled, but had the sting of truth to it too. Daniel tried to imagine fighting six Kobolds, small creatures wielding a single weapon, able to attack them from both sides in the same set up. In his full armor, he probably would have been fine, though he would have been injured. Their shivs were good at punching through gaps, though the plate mail he wore these days would have saved him.

Without his armor, without his weapons and being forced to reach for them? Daniel considered the question again, turning over the scenario in his mind. In the end, he had to assume that he probably would have won, what with the Kobolds being smaller than him and lighter. Still, a few good stabs would likely have happened, and if he was unlucky, he might have died.

"I see you're paying attention now," Lady Marshall said.

"I'm sorry, I should have foreseen this." Lady Nyssa apologized the moment she stepped into the room, Charles right behind her. The bodyguard was eyeing the surroundings idly, though Daniel noticed that he was carrying his sword on him, his hand resting on the hilt. He had also slipped on a heavy woolen tunic even in the muggy heat of the evening.

"Why would you have thought of it, when no one else did?" Daniel said.

"Yes, why?" Asin's own question was more pointed, angry.

"Because I'm your political expert. I'm the noble here. I should have foreseen something like this," Lady Nyssa said. She looked angrily at the vice-guildmaster, and then at Daniel. "I just didn't realize they were this desperate. They had offered . . ." She shook her head, dismissing her statement.

"What did they offer you?" Daniel asked. He hadn't wanted to ask before, respecting her privacy. Respecting all of his friends' privacy.

But politeness had disappeared after the beating. Somewhere between the tenth and twentieth minute, he would assume.

"Nothing of import." Asin hissed at the woman, obviously interested. Lady Nyssa relented, continuing, "Just your usual bribes. Loans, at first. Then some land, trade agreements with a few merging houses that they controlled. More land, housing, and in the end, they even offered some enchantments."

Lady Marshall nodded, obviously having expected something of the same as the answer. The vice-guildmistress turned, listening to the speakers as they came in to report on Omrak's location. Which, so far, seemed to be out of the guildhall. Additional orders were barked as guild members were sent to look for the Northerner.

"And what did they offer you?" Lady Nyssa sniped.

"Money. No beatings." Asin just shrugged. It was obvious that she had not considered any of these offers important. "Me hiding. Beastkin quarters. No come."

"Wish I had thought of that." Daniel shook his head, rotating his shoulder absolutely. It had dislocated at some point, trying to fight them off again, and he still thought he felt the pain even though his Gift itself had told him he'd fixed all the injuries. "What are we going to do about them? I never thought they'd actually hurt . . . me." Daniel felt a little bit ashamed now, now that he had said it out loud. Even though he knew Zef had been assaulted, somehow he had believed he was protected.

"And you will not remove your friends from contention?" Lady Marshall asked. Daniel just looked at her, and she laughed. "Do not look at me like that, child. You might be valuable, but I am not one of your teammates."

Daniel ducked his head, understanding what she meant. Giving the vice-guildmistress a dirty look, someone who was in the master ranks, was probably not in his best idea. He quickly apologized, and the guildmistress waved his words away.

"It is a legitimate question, and while I believe Asin and I know the answer, it would be comforting to hear you say it," Lady Nyssa said.

"I will not be letting any of my friends go. If you wish to leave, I will not stop you. I'm sure, whatever they can offer is well worth considering in most cases," Daniel said firmly. "But I do not betray my friends."

"And that is why leaving would be foolish," Lady Nyssa said.

"Mercenary," Asin said. There was no rancor in her words though, instead it was almost admiring.

Again, Lady Nyssa shrugged an elegant shoulder. "Well, it's good to know. But I think, more importantly, we should consider what we should do about these thugs. And their employers."

***

The group discussed the question of revenge over the next hour over a platter of sandwiches, brought in when Daniel noted his need for sustenance. The conversation drifted a little, going round in circles as they found their first major roadblock—a lack of knowledge of who it was that had hired Daniel's attackers. The vice-guildmistress had barked additional orders, setting the entire Guild into a frenzy as they deployed the considerable resources of the Guild to locate this information. Asin had slipped out too, returning after twenty minutes, having activated the Beastkin whisper network. Even Lady Nyssa had sent Charles to find out more, leaving Daniel to feel a little out of place. For all his skills, he had no such connections in this city. Perhaps if he had time, he might have made friends among the non-Adventuring groups while working at the hospice, but he had no such thing.

That hour of roundabout conversation ended when a commotion at the front doors brought the group out of their room. Through the front doors, a sextuplet of Adventurers stumbled in, Omrak among them. They were loud and boisterous, dirty and a little bloody with Omrak being the most injured. A large, egg-shaped swelling had appeared on his forehead and he cradled one bloody and bandaged arm.

"What happened?" Lady Marshall snapped.

"Guildmistress!" The erstwhile blue-haired leader snapped to attention, twinkling dark eyes sobering. "We found Adventurer Omrak as requested being set upon by some thugs. He was being beaten like a pig in a barrel and—"

"There were a dozen of them!" Omrak protested.

"—and we came to his rescue," the woman finished, ignoring Omrak's protests. She stepped to the side, and two more figures, bound and gagged, were shoved forwards, their presence having been hidden by the group before this. "We brought a couple back, the ones that could still talk."

"You killed them, Jupyter?" Lady Marshall frowned in disapproval.

"No, ma'am. But most were unconscious, concussed or jaws broken. Three couldn't walk, so we decided not to drag them back," Jupyter said, smiling at Omrak admiringly. "The big one's quite strong and wasn't holding back when we dragged them off. Shocked them all with this lightning thing he did."

Lady Marshall winced. "We'll have to smooth things over with the guards then."

"We left Byron behind to talk to them." That made the Lady Marshall take on a rueful look, one mixed with contained exasperation. "It's okay. He promised to be good."

"As if that ever stopped him before. Still, another infatuated guard lieutenant chasing him around is better than the guard captain," Lady Marshall muttered. "Bring these two to the cellars. I'll send Zaritska to speak with them."

The more experienced guild members all winced, while Daniel leaned over to a nearby spectating guild member and muttered, "How do they know that Byron is fine with the lieutenant? What if it's a guy?"

"It's fine." The guild member flashed a grin. "The only problem is if they're married. Then it gets tricky. Byron's quite, quite charming."

"He's a slut!" Jupyter called out, having heard the guild member's whispered reply to Daniel. Fixing her gaze on Daniel, she waved a hand at him, one that he only now realized held a broken finger hastily strapped to another. "Now, do you mind . . . ?"

"Of course!" Daniel waved the team in while others took hold of the two prisoners to bring them down to the cellars. A part of him wanted to know what would happen below, but a much wiser and older part knew that it was better not to ask.

Some things would push the boundaries of what his own code as a healer could bear.

Healing the group was a simple matter of applying his **Healer's Mark** spell, since none of them were significantly injured. In fact, Daniel was certain a few of the injuries being touted as coming from their most recent battle were a little too old, but he did not begrudge them a chance to bring themselves back to full health. They had helped Omrak, after all.

Coming to his friend at the end, he tested out the Northerner's arm, holding it carefully as he spoke. "I'm sorry. We should have told you . . ."

"Nothing to be sorry about, Friend Daniel!" Omrak rumbled. "Curs like that will gather always around the strong. It is but for us to ensure their wills are broken properly."

"And if they refuse to learn?" Daniel said.

"Then we put them down," Lady Nyssa said, coldly. "You cannot be weak at such times. Such individuals and their lackeys are quick to attack those who give in. Only strength matters to them."

Daniel could not help but frown. He wanted to protest such thoughts, but he also knew that Lady Nyssa had more experience in such things. Interpersonal conflicts for him had been mostly against other mining teams or the mine owners and in all such cases, no one ever tried to kill one another. Not when high-Level Miners with their specialized Skill Proficiencies could walk off the job and find work in another mine in a heartbeat.

Turning his attention away from the plotting, Daniel sent his Gift into Omrak's arm. A small chip of bone had broken off, pulling away into the muscles around. Using his Gift, he pushed it back into position and then pulsed his Gift, focusing it just on the bone itself. While his spells could heal the burst blood vessels and bruising, the muscle tears and cuts, bone was much tougher. Better to use his Gift here, where he might just lose a few moments of his life than spend the rest of his Mana.

Omrak hissed a little as the healing effects took place before the man stepped back, allowing his magic to do the rest of his work. The Northerner offered a smile to the healer before stepping away. Daniel, exhausted from the day's events, made his way to a chair and slumped in it, taking an offered cup of water from Asin with thanks. Soon enough, the group took their own seats, breaking into hushed conversation as they waited for information to flow back.

Watching and listening, Daniel felt his eyes grow heavy and promised himself that he was just going to close his eyes for a moment. Soon enough, his rumbling snores filled the greeting room, exhaustion and Mana overuse taking him into that languid land of dreams and honey.

Chapter 14

"Daniel. It's time to wake up."

A familiar voice, a hand shaking him. Daniel's eyes creaked open, their edges slightly gummy from lack of water. He rubbed at his face, trying to clear the sleep from his eyes as he sat up, realizing from the cracks in his hands that daylight had arrived. Pulling his head away from his hands, he looked around to see Lady Nyssa stepping back, a half-smile on her lips.

"I'm sorry. I know it's been a long night, but we have information now and decisions to be made," the noblewoman said.

Daniel sighed but stood up, his bones cracking a little as he stretched. He noted the glasses of lightly watered ale and water nearby and made his way over, pouring himself a cup as he stretched his neck from side to side.

"What news?"

"Thugs hired. Brought in hirer. Names, records, details," Asin answered from her spot by the window, looking out on the surrounding streets.

Daniel managed not to jump, not having noticed the entirely too still Catkin. He made sure to look around again, spotting Charles standing by the door silently but not seeing Omrak or any of the other Adventurers. When he turned to ask, Lady Nyssa beat him to it.

"He's just getting breakfast for us."

As if he knew he was being spoken about, the Northerner came in, backing into the room with a tray in his hands. He spun around and placed the overly-filled serving tray onto the side table, slices of bacon, sausages, fruits and bread heaped on it.

"I come bearing repast! Dire plots should only be hatched on a full stomach, my father always said," Omrak rumbled before he snatched a piece of bread and began heaping the meats on it.

"Your father take part in a lot of dire plots?" Charles asked, head tilted curiously. He did not move from his spot even as the rest of the team converged on the meal.

"Mmmm, every year as the fall ends and winter comes," Omrak said.

Daniel and Asin both stared at Omrak while Lady Nyssa cut in, swallowing her latest mouthful of food quickly. "The Northerners have a tradition of raids and pranks on the night before winter. They believe doing so, setting up traps and pranking one another, will drive the pranking monsters and spirits away since they aren't required."

Daniel frowned. "Pranking monsters?"

"Mmm, the ujomsa, the wersa, the azzul," Omrak said.

"I've never heard of them . . ." Daniel said.

"Food," Asin interrupted, waving the roll of meat and bread in her hand in front of Daniel. "Real problems, now."

Daniel grimaced, but had to agree. He scarfed down the meal, the group choosing to keep silent until they finished.

Eventually he sat back, crossing his hands over a replete stomach. "Now, tell me. What happened?"

It seemed a lot. While he had been sleeping, the full force of the Guild and the party's network had proceeded to dig into the attacks. Initially, it had not achieved much headway until Omrak's assailants had broken. After that, the Guild had managed to locate and round up

Daniel's assailants in quick order, with Asin's friends in the Beastkin community providing much of the information for bolt-holes. In particular, the manager and go-between had been found by them and dragged back personally by Lady Marshall herself.

Now, the entire group was being held by the Guild quietly in an off-site location and watched over by trusted members of the Guild. At that point, the vice-guildmistress had appeared.

"Now, we need to discuss our next steps. Dealing with your local thugs is one thing. The Watch might be upset with us for taking matters into our own hands but will only voice their opinion. The true culprits though . . ." Lady Marshall trailed off at the end.

"Do we know who they are?" Daniel said.

"The descriptions of the servants used were known to a few more of my associates," Charles said. "It seems the attacks were separately orchestrated. Though, amusingly, through one individual. It seems Amadiel had cornered the market for thugs for nobles."

"I . . . see," Daniel said, even though he truly did not.

"The issue is knowing who the nobles are has not made it any easier," Lady Marshall said, sighing. "The trio of nobles involved include two major noble houses and a minor one. We can"—she nodded over to Lady Nyssa who smiled grimly— "handle the minor house. But the major ones . . ."

"What exactly is the difference?" Daniel said.

"Mmm, a matter of influence, wealth, and Levels," Lady Marshall said. "It's not, of course, an actual designation, but a question of social standing and belief. There are some houses that have so much power their inclusion is guaranteed in such a listing, but for many, their standing is more . . ."

"Uncertain," Lady Nyssa supplied.

"Subject to change," Charles said.

Daniel shook his head, recalling previous conversations about this very topic now. They'd glossed over it, just like it was now, but he was remembering the names now that he was considering the matter. "Which houses?"

"The Iris and the Tarth," Lady Marshall said. Daniel winced, while Omrak and Asin looked puzzled. Turning to the pair, the guildmistress continued to explain. "The Iris are fair-weather allies of the royal family. They hold their place due to their wealth and lands, including a pair of Beginner Dungeons. Due to their ownership, their extended family all are, at minimum, Advanced Adventurers, having graduated through their holdings. They have a surplus of wealth too and minor enchanted items, again, drawn from the Dungeons."

"The Tarth are more concerning," Charles said, adding his own thoughts. "They are known to be antagonistic to the royal family and host the third largest standing army in the nation." Of course, Daniel knew that did not mean much. Brad did not keep much of a standing army, preferring to rely on their Adventurers. "I'm uncertain of their motives for wanting their scions in our party."

"A change of heart?" Lady Nyssa said, questioningly.

"Or something more sinister," Omrak said. "Slipping a blade into one's back is easier if you are close."

Lady Marshall shook her head. "Such speculation, even spoken here, is dangerous. Still, the question is, what should we do?"

Of course, they batted around suggestions after that. Approaching the noble groups directly was raised and dropped, since as a Guild they just did not have the strength to force the nobles to stop. Even their evidence was shaky as best, and the nobles would just ignore them without something truly convincing. Public denouncement faced the same issues and the Watch would be unable to do much without direct and clear evidence. Violence, raised by Asin, would just lead to sanctions by the Adventurers Guild and potentially even have the Guild kicked out.

Eventually, Daniel asked a simple question. "Why don't we just tell the royal family?"

"Hmmm?" Lady Marshall said, pausing. "What?"

"Among nobles, telling the royal family anything is unheard of," Lady Nyssa supplied. "It's kind of like using a Holy Sword against an undead skeleton. Overkill and liable to cause as much damage to the Dungeon, your party and the surroundings."

Lady Marshall nodded while Asin piped up. "Royals bad. Attention on high. Bad."

"Except we have their attention already," Daniel said. "So why don't we use it?"

The guildmistress made another humming noise, making Daniel look at her. At his frown, she shook her head. "Out the mouth of babes .. ." She opened her hands. "Very well. Let us try that. It might have consequences we might not foresee, though."

"Well, the consequences of ignoring their demands are quite foreseeable and dangerous." Daniel nodded over to Omrak, who had fallen asleep, bored from all the political talk and drained from the healing.

"As you said. Let us wake the griffin, then."

***

Daniel stalked the living room back and forth, back and forth. He moved in a pendulum motion, never ending as he waited. After his fifty-eighth circuit, he snarled and threw his hand up and shouted, "What the hell is going on? What's taking so long?"

"Talk," Asin replied succinctly.

"I know that!" Daniel growled, irritated. "We should be in there. These are our lives they're dealing with."

Asin shrugged in reply, making Daniel growl again in frustration. When he continued to stalk the floor, she waited until he was nearly at the other end of the room before she threw her knife, watching it lodge in the wall with a quiver. That startled Daniel, making him twirl to the side and raise his hand to shield himself, stopping only when he realized he was not wearing his shield.

"What was that for? You could have hit me!" Daniel said.

"Wouldn't." Asin sniffed, her snout wrinkling a little as her tail continued to lazily sway behind her as she crouched on the edge of the couch. "You train. Better than . . . fret. Like new mother."

"Did you just compare me to a new parent?" At Asin's nod, Daniel shook his head firmly. "Aren't you worried? Concerned about what they're talking about. Why it's taking so long?"

"Yes." Asin held up a hand before he could continue. "Can't change. Should train. Can change. Get better."

Daniel gritted his teeth, only for Lady Nyssa to approach him and put a hand on his arm. "Asin's right. We should be training. If nothing else, you learning to work without your weaponry would be good if you found yourself in the same situation as last night."

"I won't . . ."

"You cannot guarantee that," Charles, standing by the doorway, cut in. "They could come at night, in your bedroom. When you are with a young lady. Or if you're in the palace. We do not get to choose when we get to be attacked at times. Better to train."

Daniel grunted, and Omrak walked over, throwing a hand around Daniel's and Lady

Nyssa's shoulders. "Come. Asin has the way of it. There is much I can show you of the way we fight. I was my village's wrestling champion twice before I left."

Daniel sighed, his nose wrinkling a little at the smell his friend emanated, but he did let himself get pulled along. Asin was right, he might as well train while they waited. It was certainly better than wearing a hole through the carpet.

***

"Champion, was it?" Daniel said, half bent over as he caught his breath. Part of it was being thrown multiple times to the ground in the training arena. The other part was the laughter that kept threatening to bubble out of him as Omrak clambered to his feet and the affronted look he had on his face.

"I was!" Omrak paused and added, "It might have been among the children, but I was good." He glared at his opponent. "But they're always better."

"I'd say decent," said Lady Nyssa, who stepped back a little, opening up the distance between herself and the larger Northerner as he stood up. "You have the basics of your wrestling style down. However, you are out of practice and rely on your strength too much."

"And why do you know so much about wrestling?" Daniel said, frowning.

"I do come from an Adventuring family, Daniel." Lady Nyssa raised one elegant shoulder, then ducked low as Omrak tried to take advantage of her distraction to grab her. She slipped under his arm and twisted, pulling and twisting. He managed to overpower her grip and keep his feet, but she landed a foot on his backside as he stumbled past her. "We trained in unarmed combat as children."

"Children only?" Asin asked, head tilted to the side. The Catkin had declined to work on her wrestling, flashing her claws in answer when asked why. After consideration, none of the team felt the need to test how much damage she could do with those all-too-sharp instruments.

"Mmm . . . weapons and magic are much more useful. And while there are humanoid monsters, non-humanoid ones are more common. Wrestling and fighting them, unarmed, is often a losing proposition," Lady Nyssa said. "We still train with it as a refresher course, but the preference is to stay within one's specialization."

"What my lady is refusing to say is that she was uncommonly gifted," Charles said from the side where he had been coaching the group and throwing Daniel around when he had recovered. "If not for the lack of versatility in unarmed combat in most group tactics, she might have even specialized in it."

"You exaggerate," Lady Nyssa said, ducking a pair of punches that Omrak sent her way and then sending one herself to push him away. The strike was light enough that it only rocked him back a bit, forcing her to backpedal as he swung again. "It's also incredibly unladylike."

Daniel chuckled, watching as she continued to play with Omrak. It was not entirely one-sided, since a moment later, Omrak managed to feint a strike and catch her counter, using it to lever her to her knees. She attempted a roll at which point he kneed her in the ribs, releasing her arm as he did so rather than hold onto it and potentially dislocate her shoulder. Even then, the noblewoman sprawled on the ground, catching her breath.

"Nicely done, Omrak!" Daniel cheered his friend on. He had been thrashed by the pair soon after they started, which was why he was relegated mostly to working on the basics with Charles.

"Well, it seems you've gotten your breath back, good sir. Come," Charles said, interrupting Daniel and his observances. Wincing, the Adventurer turned and put his hands up. A second later, the pair were engaged, busy throwing punches, kicks, and the occasional jab while Charles coached Daniel on his footwork and timing.

In the meantime, Asin threw her knives at a convenient target, keeping an eye on the surroundings. The Catkin's nose wrinkled occasionally, her ears swiveling as she took in the noises and scents of the training yard around. Watching over the group while they waited. And if she could not shake the feeling that they might need all the training they could get, well, it might just be because she was cautious by nature and training

Chapter 15

To their surprise, not much happened over the next few days. The conversation with the prince had been short and succinct once the initial social aspects were completed. The prince and his people had left soon after the conversation had finished, and the Guild had taken pains to announce that Daniel would be taking his time to consider matters at the behest of the guildmaster.

After which, a tense silence had fallen over the proceedings. The Adventuring team had chosen to stay in the guildhall, training with one another constantly and improving their skills while they waited to hear from the royal family. Without knowing what or how the royal family intended to react to this news, the entire team were forced to wait.

It left a lot of time for Daniel to regret his suggestion. To realize that he had gone from wanting to not rely on his Gift for his Adventuring life to being forced to use its pull to make the royal family side with him. That he had, without meaning to, entangled himself even further in kingdom politics. That if they had not paid attention to him before, now they were certain to do so.

Yet for all his regrets, there was little enough that he could do to change matters. The past was what it was, leaving him with only the dull, dragging present. He found himself short-tempered and frustrated, prone to lashing out and careless in his actions. More than once, he'd been forced to heal an injury he accidentally created or received due to his attention lapsing. In the end, even Charles's infinite patience had been worn away and he had been sent off the fields.

Leaving him alone to attempt to read more works of medicine and stew in his thoughts. As daylight ended and the room he sat within on the top floor of the guildhall grew dark, Daniel chose not to move, instead glaring out at the city before him. Sending dark thoughts and petulant anger at being trapped, after all his care and desire to not be.

Caught in his own dark thoughts, Daniel never noticed her presence until she set the plate of warm food beside him. She deposited a mug of ale along with it, startling Daniel from his thoughts. He stared at the woman for a long moment, blinking a little as he noticed she had let her hair loose. The rising moon framed her face for a second, softening normally hard features.

"This . . . what . . . ?" Daniel said, struggling to pull his thoughts back to the present.

"Supper," Lady Nyssa said. "We noticed you hadn't eaten. And Asin's still smarting over what you said to her, so she didn't want to bring it up."

Daniel winced, remembering how he had accused her of just being with the team to get more money. He had been lucky she had chosen not to hit him with the knife she had been holding, though it had been a close thing.

"I should apologies to her," Daniel said.

"You should," Lady Nyssa said, then gestured to a seat beside Daniel. He nodded, a little warily as she sat beside him. "But it seems your irritation has more than impatience as its root cause."

Daniel shook his head, not wanting to answer. Instead, he turned his attention to the food, tearing into the steak and potatoes while his teammate just sat silently, staring out the window. After a few seconds, she stood up, making Daniel breathe out in relief, only to realize that she was walking around the room turning on the Mana lights. Afterwards, she returned to her seat.

Eventually, his supper was finished and he had no reason to not answer her. Beyond his own reluctance. And, Daniel realized, it was less than he had assumed. In fact, a portion of him wanted to tell someone.

"It's . . . just, I'm angry. With what happened. With how I was attacked and how I reacted. But more than that, I'm angry with myself for putting myself in this position," Daniel said, finally. He stared out the window, watching the clouds drift and block off the moon, casting them in further darkness that was only relieved by the Mana lights. "I should have done better. Should have made sure not to put myself in such a position."

"And what position is that?" Lady Nyssa probed.

"One requiring me to rely on the Guild. On the royal family," Daniel said. "One where everyone knows about my Gift."

"And its Price?" Lady Nyssa said, her lip quirking.

Daniel winced, and nodded. That to had come out, at least to the royal family and his team. "Yes."

"It was always going to come to this, you know," she said.

"True, but it could have been later. Much later."

"Then why didn't you take more precautions?"

"I . . ." Daniel paused, breathed. "I . . . couldn't." Patient silence filled the room while he struggled with the question. Till he chose to speak. "I couldn't not use this. It's a Gift. Erlis gave it to us, to us few, because she believed it needed using. It needed to be here, in this world. To turn away from it, to treat only those who I wanted . . ." He shook his head. "I'd be no better than them."

"Them?"

Daniel laughed, touching his temple. "Would you believe me if I said I don't know who they are?" Rueful, bitter laughter. "I can't remember. I just know, I just know . . ." His voice hitched. "I can't be like them. Not ever."

She looked puzzled, then seeing the pain he was in, reached out and put a hand on his arm. He stared down at it, and then upwards to the woman. Once more, he remembered she was quite pretty. There was even a small smile on her lips, before she pulled her hand back.

Perhaps there might have been something there. If she had not been a noblewoman. If he had not been a commoner. If either were higher in their careers, where strength excused much. If . . . but neither one of them were.

Lady Nyssa stood up, picking up the plate with her. She stepped back when Daniel stood, offering him a sad half-smile. "You chose, and I'd like to think you chose well. I don't think you could be who you are, the man that we all trust and follow and choose differently, Daniel." She shook her head. "The wrong choices you think you made? They also made you the man you are. And it's a good man.

"One of the better ones I've ever known."

She swept out, leaving Daniel with those words and the lingering trace of her perfume. Leaving him to stare into the night and think.

And wait, still.

***

"Kobold fool," the voice hissed into Daniel's ear, jerking him awake. He flailed with one hand, his body contorting on the chair he had been seated in. He fell off the padded chair, his arm striking nothing even as he pried gummy eyes open. Only to find a Catkin perched a short distance away on the arm of the couch, staring down at him with a grin on her lips.

"You did that on purpose," Daniel said as he pulled himself to his feet, rubbing his aching bum.

A nod and a big, sharp-toothed grin.

"Fine. I deserved it." Another nod. "But that's all you get." A frown. "But I'll buy one of those sandwiches you like. Extra spice." A grin. "Now, did you wake me up for fun or . . . ?"

Asin hopped off the couch, landing with nary a sound and strolled to the door. As she walked away, she called out behind her.

"Come."

Rolling his eyes, Daniel followed. He really wished he spoke Beastkin better, but the language had quite a few words that just did not work well with a human mouth. There were Skills that helped, of course, but he was not going to use a Skill Proficiency to improve his language acquisition.

Daniel found the team gathered near the staircase on the ground floor waiting for him and Asin. Before he could ask for more information, Asin pushed him towards the washroom, muttering "Breath" so softly that he almost missed it.

Cleaned and bereft of a breath that could knock out a troll from fifty paces, Daniel stood before them all, arms crossed. "Well?"

"We're going to the royal palace," the guildmaster said, strolling out from deep within the mansion. Unlike the others, he was dressed to the nines today which meant extra tight breeches, a roll of socks down the front of his pants, and extra floppy sleeves on his tunic.

Omrak's jaw dropped a little at the sight of the guildmaster while the other team members did their best to keep their faces straight, especially when the guildmaster met their gazes and dared them to say anything.

"Now, where is she . . ." As if recalled, the front door opened, and the Lady Marshall strolled in. She too was wearing dresswear, in her case a flowing dress with a small corset that pushed up her chest. Luckily, current fashion required her chest to be covered, otherwise she would have put most tavern wenches to shame.

"They have their weapons?" Lady Marshall said.

"Yes," the guildmaster said. His gaze landed on Daniel, frowning. "You do have your gear, do you not?"

"I . . ."

"I have it, sir," Omrak rumbled. "Deposited in my inventory. We can dress there, no?"

"Yes. That will do." A nod and then the guildmaster swept out of the door, calling out behind him, "Well, come on then. No dragging your feet. This is a royal decree!"

Hurrying after the group, Daniel hissed, "What is going on?"

"We're not sure," Lady Nyssa replied for the team, as they all piled into the waiting pair of carriages. "We've been told to come to the palace. And that is all."

Groaning, Daniel sat within and stared down at his clothing. He had not washed, nor had he changed. Somehow, turning up to the palace in dirty clothing seemed like a bad idea. One that he raised, for which Charles had a solution. A simple spell—one that the servant had on hand—at least removed the body odor and freshened up his clothing. It still looked like the worn clothing of the mildly successful Adventurer that he was, but it was at least clean.

Even if it did nothing to help ease his anxiety at the sudden summons.

***

The group were marched into the palace shortly after they arrived, brought in by a group of guards and a single attendant. Daniel had barely any time to actually look at the palace, though he was left with a feeling of understated wealth as they finally arrived at the main hall. All around them, large tapestries of previous battles and important events—from the Sundering to the First Battle of Warmount—had been displayed as they were marched past, Mana lights lit even in the middle of the day to ensure that proper lighting was provided. Daniel had not spotted a single candle, while the presence of a large number of noblemen, servants and guards kept his head on the swivel.

The attendant barely even stopped at the doors, Daniel's and the party's presence obviously having been expected. The doors swung open, and the announcer proceeded to inform the waiting individuals within of their arrival.

The greeting hall beyond the doors was half packed with individuals, the vast majority nobles. There were some familiar faces, other adventuring nobles, including some of those that had applied for the spots in the team.

However, what drew Daniel's attention were the five individuals on the throne room's dias at the head of the hallway. Of course, they were all relatively familiar faces. The king and queen both had their heads stamped on the coins that they used every day, and Daniel had seen illustrated portraits of them before at public events. The third prince was of course quite familiar, having made his presence known at the meeting. The other two faces were familiar only in the familial resemblance manner, and consisted of the second prince and the princess. The first prince was away, working with the Army in the East.

The second prince himself was a tall, angular man, more known for his bookish tendencies than his martial prowess. Still, the fact that he was a relatively accomplished Mage kept any complaints to the minimum. As for the princess, she continued to be the baby of the family at only fourteen years of age, still too young to entertain any serious marriage offers. Not that it had stopped some nobles and neighboring countries from sending over suitors.

". . . And the healer Daniel Chai, and his party." The attendant had just finished the announcements, drawing Daniel's attention back to him upon hearing his name. He followed the guildmaster, a few steps behind, and echoed the bow that the guildmaster offered to the king.

As Daniel raised his head, he noted the gray and thinning hair, the wrinkles along the king's eyes and the silver spots along his arm. The once-powerfully built king had grown thin, the vestiges of his impressive musculature continued to be seen. Beside him, dressed in similar yellow and purple-colored formal attire, was the queen. She, unlike the king, was much younger, having married him much later, after the first king's wife had died, failing to give him an heir. The matronly brunette still offered Daniel a smile, her eyes kind as she swept over the group.

Around Daniel, he could hear the harsh murmurs of the crowd, the angry and annoyed conversations as they took offense at the presence of Asin. It did not escape Daniel's eyes that this was a very human court, not a single other Beastkin being present.

"So, this is the Gifted Healer that has caused us so much trouble." The king's gaze swept over Daniel, and he found himself unconsciously straightening his back. The Imperial Aura held by King Lassiter was a powerful Skill that included the entirety of the land, but it was most prominent in this room. "He's shorter than I expected. And brawnier."

He turned his head to the side where an older, portly man stood, his arms folded in his robes. "Tell me, Healer Rotfield, is this a new trend for Healers? Putting into effect all this proper living and exercising they preach?"

"No, your majesty. I believe the boy is an Adventurer," Rotfield said.

"I've seen Healer Adventurers; none of them are so wide," King Lassiter said.

"Hush, husband." A hand came to rest on his arm, the queen inclining her head to where Daniel had flushed a little at being so openly discussed in public. "You've embarrassed the poor boy. You know he was a Miner before."

"Yes. A Miner and then an Adventurer, while being Gifted with a healing ability that puts even our Court Healer to shame." A long, elongated pause as the king leaned forwards. "Or so it's rumored."

"Not a rumor, your majesty," Guildmaster Ronson said. "Adventurer Chai has proven that multiple times at our guildhall and at other locations."

"For me, for example," the Champion Eronin said.

Daniel and most of the audience started, turning to stare at the Champion, who somehow seemed to have faded into the background. That was a surprise, considering the Champion was a six-foot-plus scion of a man, clad in full plate armor. Yet, having stood in the back quietly till now, everyone had ignored him. Daniel peered over, and though the man was a little too far away for him to see, but he knew that a faded scar lay on the Champion's left cheek.

"Yes, I recall that particular note," King Lassiter said, gesturing for the Champion to come forward. "You even said that he'd fixed that persistent ache in your foot. That even Rotfield was unable to do anything about."

"As I've mentioned before, your majesty, old . . ."

"Old injuries are the hardest to heal and require either reinjuring the location, which is not advised with non-critical injuries, or a powerful spell which would take you many hours if not days to recover from," King Lassiter parroted. "I remember. But this young boy, with his Gift, could do so."

"Yes, he can. The Gifted can always do more than those of us can, except in the most extreme cases. That is, after all, what the Gift is about," Rotfield said, his voice cool.

"Well, I'd love to see that then," Lassiter said.

"That?" Guildmaster Ronson said.

"The Healer's Gift. I believe my wife has mentioned that she has had some persistent problems since the birth of . . . well." Eyes twinkling, the old man moved away from the fan that his wife had found, striking him in his arm. "That's not required. I'm sure he can locate the problem and fix it."

Rotfield's eyes narrowed. "Your majesty, as your Healer, I must caution you on this . . ."

"I hear you, Rotfield," King Lassiter said, cutting the man off. "But I trust Guildmaster Ronson and Champion Eronin. Now, come, Guildmaster."

"Of course." Ronson turned to Daniel, raising an eyebrow only for Eronin to speak up again.

"My Liege, there is one other side of the coin for our extraordinary Gifts . . ." he said.

"The Price. Yes. We will discuss that, but first, let us see this Gift." The King gestured again.

Daniel felt the weight of the attention of the entire court shifting to him, and he gulped. He took a step, finding his legs hard to move under all that attention. Yet he forced himself to keep walking, ascending the dais where the queen and the king sat. As he neared, the prince actually moved closer, almost standing beside his mother and Daniel. He said nothing, but the look he gave Daniel reminded the Adventurer of the stakes he was playing at.

"I need to touch you . . . your majesty," Daniel said, bowing a little.

"Is my hand sufficient?" the queen asked, holding it up.

"Yes." Daniel hesitated before forcing himself to take her hand, finding it extremely soft. He held it for a second, his body tensing as he reached within himself. His Gift, as always, was within easy reach. "This might take a second. There should not be much pain, but if there is, let me know."

"Of course."

Daniel exhaled and delved into her body. For a woman of her age, one that had given birth to four children, she was in very good shape. In fact, there was very little wrong with her, at least not on a major level. Then again, Daniel would not expect anything else.

He sent his mind in, further and further, reaching with his Gift. There were minor issues: a bunion there, a small cluster of cells that he felt was wrong, aggressive. He killed that with his Gift with nary a thought. Then, he crossed across her organs finding her heart, her liver, her kidney. The kidneys weren't as strong as they could be, but he could work with that. A little bit of a push, a little prod.

But lower down, lower—that was where Daniel felt it. He could tell the birth had been hard. Not life-threatening, but damaging enough that the effects of torn labia and weakened muscles had persisted. If he had more details, perhaps he could have pulled together a more complete picture, but it almost felt like the multiple births and the healing spells used afterwards—or even during a birth—had exacerbated the problem.

"This . . ." Daniel trailed off, shaking his head. "I'll need to fix it by breaking it down," Daniel said. "It'll hurt a little." He paused, feeling as memories slipped away. He only had a glimpse of them, a brief fraction of a second to see what they were like. A midnight kiss, a combination strike with shield and mace, entering an outhouse . . .

"Understood. Do what you have to, Adventurer." Her voice was soft, commanding.

Daniel took a breath, then let it out as he delved within. Muscles had to be broken down, old scar tissue torn apart and rebuilt, capillaries and blood vessels stitched together again, tendons reinforced. He dove into his healing, even as he felt his memories, his very being, escape with each moment. Daniel could have made it go faster, rushed the process. With anyone else, he would have. It would have meant fewer memories lost, but in turn, the queen would have felt more pain. He chose not to, a part of him knowing that he was being watched.

He healed her, speeding the process along as fast as he could and then, slowly, pulled away. He dropped her hand, feeling a wave of exhaustion strike him before he steadied himself. Memories, the edge of what he lost raced through his mind. The taste of breakfast just the other week, the feel of a mandible crushing his leg, shattering bone. Laughter, as a night of carousing with Asin and Omrak left.

His Gift took its price and left Daniel diminished.

"And, my dear?" King Lassiter asked.

The queen tapped her chin with a single finger as Daniel was gently ushered down the dais. Her second son watched the proceedings silently, lips pursed, while the third son flashed Daniel an encouraging grin which he returned, wanly.

"I feel no major differences. Some minor changes but . . ." She shrugged.

"May I, Your Majesties?" Rotfield strode over at their nod, touching her shoulder and casting a spell. He reviewed her Status, reading the information and then, frowning, cast another spell. And another.

"Healer Rotfield?" King Lassiter said, his voice growing concerned. Guards shifted, eyeing Daniel, and one even went so far as to touch her blade hilt. "Is there something wrong?"

"No. Not at all." Rotfield shook his head. "My apologies, My Liege. I was just a little focused. . . . The Queen is in perfect health. I believe he has even managed to deal with her minor issues."

"Well, well." Lassiter smiled. "So it is true. A true miracle, and one with so little a price."

Daniel shook his head, finding in himself the anger, the courage to contradict the king. "Not little, My Liege."

"Really? And what, exactly, is this price?" the king asked, leaning forward. He saw Daniel hesitate and his voice grew colder, firmer. "Take it as a command if you will, to tell me."

"My memories," Daniel said, softly. Realizing the king had trapped him, forced him to speak about it in public. He did not want to, but he had no choice it seemed.

"Speak up, boy. I did not hear you."

"My memories." Daniel's voice grew louder, firmer.

The royal hall grew quiet at that point, before conversation broke out. Daniel caught a few snippets of conversation, his face flushing with both anger and embarrassment.

". . . memories? What kind of price is that?"

"I have a few I'd want to give."

"Do you think he can fix a limp? My uncle . . ."

"And he can cast it again? Amazing . . ."

"We should get our son with him . . ."

"He's sort of cute. Maybe Katherine might be willing . . ."

Yet, when the king spoke up, everyone grew silent, knowing better than to speak over the man. "A heavy price. We begin to see your reluctance." A pause. "Still, you will make yourself available to us, as necessary."

"As your majesty commands," Daniel said, bowing.

"Good. Now, to the reason you were brought here . . ." The king's voice dropped, his gold-blue eyes sweeping over the nobles. A number were gestured forwards by the attendants, the older gentleman and lady who headed the households unknown to Daniel. By his side, Lady Nyssa whispered their names and ranks, though Daniel found himself fighting hard to hold on to them.

For one thing, that anger at being mocked, at his secret being revealed combined with the sight of his tormentors, the young men who had insisted on joining his group. Three of them, two who were familiar—Lord Zaynastra the Duelist and Lord Biber. The third was one that had not even made an impression on Daniel, a younger Lord Nicholas whose greatest distinguishing characteristic was his lack of them.

"It seems your activities have created some disturbance in my city. So much so that you have involved my sons." King Lassiter's voice dropped. "I dislike being bothered about such matters, and dislike my family being used as . . . pieces in another's play."

"Your majesty, we would never . . ." The thin, goateed leader of the nobles spoke up, the blousy yellow jacket he wore adorned with creeping irises of his house. He dared to even cut off the king, speaking while the other took a breath. "These accusations are unfounded and without evidence."

"Very much without evidence." Another nobleman, the designated leader of House Tarth in the city, spoke up from his place just behind the goateed nobleman. He had deep-set, weaselly eyes and a way of looking around that made Daniel think of a rat.

"There have been a spate of killings in our capital recently. Thugs, a broker and his men and, I hear, your servants." The king's voice grew cold. "Coincidence, I assume?"

"No, your majesty," the goateed Iris house leader said. "I believe it to be action taken to frame my house by these . . . peasants." He looked over at Guildmaster Ronson, Lady Marshall, and Daniel, sneering. "For the murder of my men, I demand that justice be dealt."

"I agree," the weaselly man said.

"And you, Lady Brooke? Does House Quinn have an opinion?" King Lassiter said.

"We agree," the Lady Brooke replied. Her hands were wrapped around the edges of her skirt, bunching them up as she spoke, but her voice was steady. Treading in deep waters or not, she managed to at least sound confident, if not look it.

"I see. And so, here we are," King Lassiter said. "But the problem is, as you said, we have no evidence. In either direction."

There were nods from the group of noblemen, forcing Daniel to growl. At least they had not gone so far as to trot out false witnesses. It would have been difficult anyway, what with truth stones and Peacekeepers able to discern the truth. It might be viable to conduct such fraud in other cities, but the king had access to significantly more resources than a local magistrate.

"No, your majesty. I'm sure some of those killed were their accomplices." Again, the Iris househead sneered.

Daniel gritted his teeth, his anger threatening to erupt.

The king swept his gaze over Daniel, noting his reactions and those of his party who were just as incensed, before his lips twisted into a wry smile. "It seems we are at an impasse."

"Perhaps. But I have a recommendation," the weaselly man said, his voice oozing charm and slime. At the king's gesture, he continued. "I suggest we resolve this traditionally. Trial by combat between our noble houses and the Three Stones Guild. After all, I do not think the healer would take such action."

"I see, Lord Barber. And you have, of course, thought of what you will get if you win."

"We only desire some minor things. Removal of the Healer from the Seven Stones Guild. They are, obviously, a bad influence. We'll make sure to ensure he and the prince are properly managed," Lord Barber said, touching his chest. "Access to his Gift, of course, for the damage caused to our reputation."

"Is that all?" Daniel said, unable to stop himself from speaking. "Dismissing my party and working for you for free?!"

"Quiet! Even a lowly peasant like you should know better than to interrupt their king!" Lord Barber snapped.

"And you should learn to speak properly to the Gifted," the Champion rumbled, hand on the hilt of his sword. "He is no simple peasant, and you would be wise to remember that."

Lord Barber turned, a sneer on his lips that he smoothed out after a second. "Of course. I misspoke. Though the . . . Healer . . . should know better."

Daniel moved to speak further, only to be silenced as Lady Marshall touched his arm. When he looked at her, she shook her head while

Guildmaster Ronson requested to speak. Receiving the king's agreement, he spoke up.

"We categorically deny any wrongdoing in this matter, but we do agree that a trial by combat is the simplest method to deal with this issue. However, I note that this is very one-sided in penalties. When the Seven Stones Guild wins, compensation for besmirching our name and for the attacks will be required."

"Just like a merchant, always looking for money," the Iris Houseleader said. He waved a dismissive hand. "House Iris will cover whatever coin or good penalties that might arise as judged by your majesty in the event we lose."

"Well, that seems simple enough," King Lassiter said, smiling as he leaned forwards. "A trial by combat to settle matters." He paused, his gaze sweeping over the group, House Iris and Tarth already gesturing towards their own men to come forward to act as champions. "But since this entire situation started with the Healer and his party and your sons, they will be the participants in this duel. None other."

"Your majesty . . . !"

Protests rang out, but the king gestured, cutting them off.

"I have spoken. Captain of the Guard—make ready our training grounds. We shall see this matter settled. Today."

Chapter 16

To Daniel's disgust, they were led away through the palace to a sprawling, highly equipped sparring grounds. The space itself was triple the size of the training grounds the Seven Stones Guild had in Silverstone and could easily rival the size of the Adventurers Guild's own training center. Except unlike the Adventurers Guild's training center, which was packed with Adventurers at all hours of the day, this particular training ground was empty, bereft of individuals.

No surprise, since it was the royal family's personal training ground. Still, it grated on Daniel since all that space, all those weapons lining the weapon racks, the enchanted spells and the glowing runes that kept individuals safe and could create copies of monsters, all of that were wasted most days. Left to just lie, unused.

"Now, seeing that there are four of you Adventurers but only three challengers, one of you will have to choose to step aside," the king said. He smirked a little, gaze flicking over the group before he continued. The nobles stirred, some moving to object while the king spoke up. "There is no fear about death here. The Royal

Healer and, of course, Adventurer Chai are both here to heal any injuries, while the enchantments in our training grounds will protect against any immediately fatal blows. Unless, of course, you don't believe the enchantments we have are adequate."

Of course, all the nobles and attendants were quick to assure the king that the royal enchantments which protected the royal family were more than sufficient. Nodding along, King Lassiter cut them off once he was satisfied.

"Then there are no objections, are there?"

The last was a rhetorical question, obviously. However, to everyone's surprise, there was a response. It came from Lord Biber, his voice dripping with scorn. "Only that we are being forced to fight such creatures. That our word, as noblemen, is weighted to the same extent as these peasants."

"Now, you are correct." The king said. "You are my nobles, the individuals most trusted in my reign. It should be impossible for you to lie. But this is a trial of combat and the speaker, a Gifted. It will be overseen by Erlis herself.

"Still, I can perceive your concerns. I understand them. So I will rule this. The Adventurers will have to win all the fights, for this their accusations to hold. But, if they succeed, I will strip every noble son who stands on the field of combat of their rights as nobles. Your parents will have to find a new heir."

Lord Biber's jaw dropped open, even as Lord Barber, standing next to the boy, winced. Unfortunately, there was nothing he could do, for the king had spoken. And, as his gaze tracked over to Daniel's group, he could see that they too were unhappy with the pronouncement.

"Now, I think I should leave you all to begin your preparations. In fifteen minutes, send out the first of your combatants." King Lassiter finished speaking and then strolled away, heading for the pair of chairs that had been hastily set aside for him and his wife. The other members of the royal family were also found smaller, less elaborate chairs to sit upon, and spectate the upcoming fight. Everyone else was forced to stand.

***

Quickly enough, attendants drew Daniel and his team aside. Guildmaster Ronson followed along with them, casually eyeballing the nobles who were headed to their own corner of the training arena. Even now, Ronson noticed how Lord Biber was berating the team, obviously less than impressed with the results of the king's choice. Then again, he was the main heir to the House of Biber and as such had the most to lose. As for the small, slight boy who was all too average, he slunk along behind, in silence.

In short order, the entire group were assured of two changes to their equipment. The Adventurers had all carried their gear under his instructions, and so was only a matter of being dressed. The nobles however took a little longer, arguing among themselves and they sought to make use of the weapons offered to them. All but the Duelist, who refused anything but his own equipment that he brought out from his own storage ring.

Drawing a deep breath, Guildmaster Ronson confirmed in his mind what needed to be done. Already, the kids were back and speaking to one another. Lady Marshall, he had sent off, on the off-chance that things went badly for them. Whatever happened today, there was bound to be some retaliation against their Guild.

"I shall be doing battle," Omrak grumbled. "I should be the first. Once we have beaten their best, the rest will be simple."

"You think you are good enough to beat the Duelist?" Lady Nyssa shook her head. "He'd take you apart long before you even managed to hit him. This is exactly the kind of fighting that he is used to."

"Yes, dangerous," Asin said. The Catkin was crouched slightly, fingers playing across the bandolier of knives she had slipped on, checking each of them over.

"Perhaps, before you consider who should be fighting, you should consider what you are facing," Guildmaster Ronson said, his voice cutting through the trio's discussion. As he spoke, he turned the ring on his finger, using the enchantment on it to block off sight and sound of the group as they strategized. It still allowed him to watch as the nobles grimaced, obviously upset that they had not managed to acquire such an easy win.

"It's those three, isn't it?" Daniel said. "I remember the classes of the first two, Duelist and Nobleman. The noble isn't much of a challenge, other than whatever enchanted equipment he might have, but I don't remember the third."

The others shook their heads, also looking puzzled as well. Asin in particular was looking highly troubled, having gone so far as to flex the claws in her hands in and out.

"That is because he does not want you to remember." The guildmaster shook his head. "If he was not also registered as an Adventurer, and Nobleman, the Watch would have taken him in a long time ago."

"He's a thief?" Mark said.

"Worse. He's a Rogue," Master Ronson said. "At least, that's what his papers say officially. I have my doubts."

"You think he's an assassin," Lady Nyssa said. Her voice held a little bit of fear in it, and she glanced at the utterly average man and his parents.

"Assassins?" Daniel frowned. "Aren't they just children's stories? I mean, you can hire a Classed-up Rogue to kill someone, but as a Class? It doesn't seem very useful. I mean, anyone who just inspected him would know."

"Lesser Class abilities include the ability to hide such information," Guildmaster Ronson said. "But it is all speculation. At the very least, he's fast, able to hide himself and make you forget about him. He might carry a sword like the others, but you'll notice it's a little shorter than normal. I don't think that's even his primary weapon. Your only advantage against him is that this is not his arena."

"Duelist," Asin said.

"Yes, exactly. This is a Duelist arena. And in that sense, you are all at a disadvantage. Not only can you not use your teamwork in these individual bouts, but the Duelist is much stronger. And you must win all three fights."

Ronson shook his head. "You have to win, you understand that."

The group nodded grimly, before Ronson gestured at all for them. "Now, if you listen to me, I have a suggestion about who you should send out. And the order."

Finding themselves unexpectedly faced with an extremely serious guildmaster, the group hastily agreed, even as they noted how little time they had to choose. Guidance, in this case, was the best option.

***

"Her?" There was a rumble of surprise that swept through the crowd as the first member of Daniel's party stepped forward. Rather than the large Northerner that most had expected, it was the Mage who approached the dueling ring. Opposing her was the Duelist, his hand on the hilt of his sword. His eyes tracked Lady Nyssa as she walked over, eyes narrowed in consideration.

"A bold choice," Lord Zaynastra said, lips pursed. It was obvious that they had chosen to win the entire challenge quickly by sending out their best fighter.

Lady Nyssa chose not to answer the statement, instead taking her spot a short distance away at the starting positions marked on the floor. Lord Zaynastra drew his weapon, lowering his center of gravity, his sword held low but pointed towards Lady Nyssa. Daniel knew that particular stance since it was a common starting form. Highly offensive, the low point still allowed the attacker to transition to numerous guards, allowing the point to target any number of locations.

Fist clenched tight, Daniel could only stand and watch from the sidelines as the Mage got ready. In many ways, the environment of the arena put the Mage at a significant disadvantage. Her spells required casting time, but the limited size of the arena meant she had to start close to her opponent. Without a frontline to block her attacker, she had little enough time to prepare her spells and by the rules of the duel, she could not even precast the spells.

It was because of all that the other team and Lord Zaynastra were surprised by her presence. Of course, everyone knew she was a Mage and a noble, thus having some form of enchanted protection. Given enough time, she could likely turn the battle around, but it was for that reason that the Duelist was ready to charge her.

The referee, the royal family's personal Master-at-Arms stood, between the pair and off to the side, a long staff in hand. He raised it high and then dropped it, using his voice at the same time to signal the start of the duel.

Lord Zaynastra blurred, crossing the ground between the pair in three hasty steps. **Flicker Movement** was a Duelist Skill and one he was well known for, allowing a Duelist to cross the space between himself and his opponent in a flash. The action allowed him to strike first almost every time and to ensure he did not miss. Daniel noted the swirl of Mana that formed around the tip of his weapon, another Duelist Skill—**Unerring Strike** activating.

Combined, it was a deadly combination. Not impossible to beat though. **Flawless Parry** or

Shield Block were common counters to **Unerring Strike** so long as the melee fighter was able to react in time. The combination was so common among beginning duelers that few, at Lord Zaynastra's level, would even consider using it since it spent so many Skills and Stamina immediately.

However, Lord Zaynastra was not facing a melee fighter. He was dueling a Mage, and it was thus no surprise that he managed to cross the ground and land his attack without opposition. Lady Nyssa even flinched backwards, a foot rising as she attempted to pivot away even as her lips worked, starting the chant for her spell.

The *crack* of the **Unerring Strike** hammering into an enchanted shield echoed through the training grounds, bringing with it gasps from the audience. More than a few eyes noted the flaring of power on the Adventurer's necklace as it expanded its shielding charge to cover her inadequate defense.

Eyes dancing with amusement, Lord Zaynastra did not let up. He activated his third Skill of the day, **Duplicate Attack,** immediately, his hand thrusting forward with the same strength and speed as his first attack. He managed to shift the second attack slightly even as Lady Nyssa kept spinning, borrowing some of the impetus of his first attack.

Then, to his surprise and the audience, his second attack landed. The blade aimed at her shoulder had been forcibly shifted off course a little by the spin, the Skill allowing him to borrow strength and speed but not accuracy. Still, it skewered the Mage through her body, even as she completed her own attack.

Leg raised, instead of being used to step aside, it was used to kick outwards. It caught the Duelist in his ribs, pushing him and cracking a rib, surprising the man as much for the kind of attack as the sacrifice she had made. Then, foot falling back to the ground, never having stopped weaving her spell, the Mage raised her hand.

Again, Lord Zaynastra darted forward, but this time, he was too late. Injured or not, the Mage—a Battle Mage in truth—had managed to complete her spell. And while the Duelist might have managed to dodge or dance aside from any other attack, utilizing his Skills to avoid most attacks—the **Shrieking Orb** that Lady Zaynastra unleashed struck the entirety of the arena.

Outside, the buzz of her attack was just a low-edged hum to Daniel's ears. The enchantments around the dueling ring were sufficient to dampen the attack. Within, though, Lord Zaynastra staggered backwards, bones and skull shook, ears burst and balance robbed of him. It was testament to the enchantments he too carried that he had not fallen immediately, receiving the full brunt of the Mage's channeled attack. Even injured, the Duelist pushed forwards, but the Mage was easily able to escape his staggering pursuit.

In short order, the battle was over, the outcome no longer in contention. Only when the shielding around the arena had dropped did Daniel rush forwards to his friend, only to be beat to the healing by the Royal Healer. Daniel shot him a grateful glance, only to find Healer Rotfield giving him a smirking smile.

As the pair walked back to the group, Guildmaster Ronson was standing by them all, gloating. "Told you the damn Duelist would fall for it. They always think in terms of points, but we're Adventurers. We can fight through pain if we have to."

A big hand came up and clapped down on Lady Nyssa's shoulder, making her stagger and hiss out in pain. Guildmaster Ronson flashed her an apologetic smile before the Master-of-Arms called out,

"Next fighters!"

***

"This is unfair . . ." Lord Biber whimpered, sword and shield held before him. He was fully armored in plate mail, visor down, but even then, Daniel could see his legs shaking.

Asin, crouched opposite him, had a pair of throwing knives in both her hands. Crouched low, the Catkin was just grinning at her opponent, her tail idly lashing out behind her in long, lazy strokes. All around them, conversations were being held, the low murmur of conversations among the audience rolling over the arena. It was obvious that few individuals had any doubts about the outcome of this fight.

"Ready?" the Master-of-arms called.

"This . . . I . . ." Another gulp by Lord Biber.

He looked to the side, meeting the firm gaze of Lord Barber, who glared at the young man. He seemed to wilt even more, which Daniel had not thought was even possible. Eventually, he managed to croak out his readiness to the waiting Master-of-Arms.

Moments later, the staff fell, and a pair of throwing knives, each of them homing in on the gaps in his defense, were flying through the air. The first struck the breastplate, clinking as it fell to the ground, the other finding a gap between thigh and groin armor. The first bounced off the armor, only light sparkles of electricity that soon grounded itself showing the purpose of her attack. The second was bounced off by a similar magical item like Lady Nyssa's.

Not to be deterred, the Catkin started stalking around the nobleman, who shuffled after her awkwardly. Occasional throwing knives would flash out, bouncing off armor or the occasional shield, imparting their short burst of charged electricity before falling to the ground. Even more rarely, the enchanted piece would flare, its power drained.

Like the patient predator that she so resembled, Asin stalked Lord Biber, attacking him and leading him around the arena. She even pathed herself back to her throwing knives, picking them up to use them again.

After the fourth time, Lord Barber screamed, "Stop letting her pick up her weapons, you idiot!"

The moving tank of plate-clad armor paused, obviously hesitating and thinking. Then, slowly, it retreated to the latest thrown knife and kicked at it, sending it out of the arena.

Asin hissed, but said nothing, while Daniel growled. "Isn't that illegal? Shouting advice?"

Guildmaster Ronson offered Daniel a tight-lipped smile. "Yes. But the king has said nothing, and so shall we."

The group gave a curt nod, obviously unhappy.

Even then, the illegal aid did little to change the flow of battle. Changing her tactics a little, the Catkin now wielded one throwing knife and her much larger fighting knife. She would throw the first knife and then dart in when Lord Biber took his eye off her to kick at the throwing knife to launch her own close-ranged attacks. Sliding to the outside of the shield or sometimes under, she'd lash out with her long-bladed knife to score armor and find gaps.

All of which were foiled by the heavy plate and the flickering enchantments. Yet the Catkin did not despair as she picked at the noble. Each of her attacks, enchanted by her bracers, did a little damage, draining the enchantment. Furthermore, unused to moving in heavy plate, Lord Biber grew slower and slower.

The fight dragged on and on, the lord never able to catch the fleet Catkin. The audience grew uneasy and bored, upset that the entire thing took so long. A few of the braver nobles even voiced their concerns out loud in the hopes that the king would say something, but King Lassiter and the royal family continued to watch the entire proceedings silently.

When the end came, it came in a flash. Asin threw her remaining throwing knife, the weapon flashing through the air to be blocked by a raised shield. As the shield was brought up high and blocked his vision, she darted forwards without a sound and then gripped the shield. Pulling it one way and twisting herself on the outside, she proceeded to slam the hilt of her knife into the extended arm and shoulder blade of her opponent.

The next second, Lord Biber was face down on the ground, arm extended fully, his weapon arm trapped under him as he had attempted to bring it around. A knee and heavy weight came down on his body, too heavy for the weak nobleman to push against.

After which the Catkin used the hilt of her weapon to strike at his helmet repeatedly until the Master-at-Arms called the fight over, spotting how the nobleman beneath her had stopped struggling.

Grinning, the Catkin hopped up and went around the edges of the arena, retrieving her throwing knives with a smile on her face that was entirely too self-satisfied.

Ashamed and embarrassed, the nobleman had to be carried off the field of battle, his Stamina entirely drained in his final struggles. Retreating to her side of the field, the Catkin surreptitiously wiped away a gob of spittle, one that had been "gifted" to her as she went retrieving her weapons.

Still, she kept silent. This was, after all, not the time. But she did mark the spitter.

Arena clear, the Master-at-Arms spoke up once more, calling the final combatants. And, as one, the team turned to stare at their last, most mysterious, of opponents.

Chapter 17

Standing opposite the Assassin, the Rogue, Daniel could not help but breathe slowly. Memories of the hurried conversation with Guildmaster Ronson flashed through his mind.

"We'll send Lady Nyssa to deal with the Duelist. He's too fast for anyone else. Yes, even you, Asin. I don't care which one of you two take Lord Biber. He's the easy win."

"Too easy. There is no honor in beating him," Omrak rumbled.

"Mine," Asin agreed.

Guildmaster Ronson glared at the pair to shut them up before he continued. "For the Assassin, that has to be Daniel."

"Why me?" he'd squeaked.

"Two reasons. Assassins do their most damage on their first attack. They cut and hit and use poisons. None of which, with your Gift and your healing, will affect you. A battle of attrition is in your favor."

Lady Nyssa frowned. "I disagree. Charles has some Skill Proficiencies that would work against him if he is what you think he is."

"That leads to my second reason," Guildmaster Ronson said. *"Of you all, Daniel is the only one he won't be willing to kill, even accidentally."*

"I thought the enchantments . . ." he had begun.

"Protect against killing blows by mitigating them. But Assassin Skills work counter to those enchantments," Guildmaster Ronson said. *"Or so I've been led to believe. I'm not willing to risk anyone else, are you?"*

And that, of course, had ended the conversation. Which, Daniel mused, led to him standing here in his own set of full plate, staring at the Rogue opposite him. The one who was crouched low, a short sword in one hand and a dagger in the other. Even standing still, something in the way he stood, in the Skill he used, made Daniel want to look away, to shift his eye for a brief second.

"Are you ready?" the Master-at-Arms called, taking Daniel's attention away for a brief second.

The Adventurer nodded and switched his attention back to the Rogue. He cursed himself for shifting his eyes away, even as the staff dropped.

Like their first opponent, Daniel chose to rush forward and cover the ground. Unlike Lord Biber though, even clad in full plate, he moved quickly and smoothly. Even the heavier iron plate armor he wore caused little issue for Daniel as he closed the distance, so used to wearing it he was.

His opponent backed off and edged sideways, intent on circling and giving himself space to work. Daniel cut him off, doing his best to hem in his opponent as he closed in. The distance was not that far, so in a half-dozen steps he had his opponent pressed to the edge of the arena.

Too easy. Even as the thought crossed his arm, Daniel pushed his shield forward to lead the way, his hammer and held behind. He used the angle of his shield to cover his outside line, his left foot leading as he waited for the surprise attack. A thrown dagger? A level change to bring the short sword cutting at his foot?

Neither, it seemed.

To Daniel's surprise, his shield pushed right through the short sword. Right through, as the temporary mirage of the Rogue's **Mirror Image** Stealth Proficiency faded. Off-balance a little and surprised even more, he never saw the attack that slipped in under his extended arm into the gap underneath his armpit.

The dagger went upwards, cutting through reinforced cloth and padding into skin and flesh, severing tendons and ligaments. His entire arm dropped, the pain arriving moments later as the dagger slipped out, its job done. Pain, and then a wave of numbness, as the poison in the blade took hold.

Daniel staggered to the side, waving his hammer to deflect any follow-up attacks. There were none, for the Rogue had stepped back, a small smile on his face as he waited for his attack to take effect. Only to be surprised when Daniel elected to throw his weapon, sending the hammer clipping off his hip as he hastily dodged.

Daniel grinned, taking the brief moment to slip into his own body with his Gift. With any other individual, he would need a few interrupted seconds to fix the issue. Every body, every individual was different but Daniel knew his own intimately. He swept the poison out of his body, letting his heart pump it out along with his blood, staining his clothing and armor before he stitched the tendons, ligaments, and blood vessels together.

His arm barely worked, but it was enough for now even as he suppressed his own pain response, pushing backwards as his opponent came for him. Hunkering in his armor, careful to not give his opponent a major opening, Daniel wove the spell form for **Healer's Mark** on himself.

"Do you think your Gift is enough?" the Rogue taunted, his voice lowered so only the pair of them could hear. "I have more poisons than you have memories. Give up now. I've killed higher-Leveled Adventurers than you."

Daniel said nothing, feeling the first wash of the spell roll over him, helping patch together the injury. As a blade clanged off his helmet, throwing his vision off a little, he punched at the arm that attacked him, clipping it a little. Then again, as he took a cut with the sword with his injured arm, he stomped on a foot, catching the edges of their toes.

All the while, trying to edge back towards his own hammer. To the weapon he had cast aside to injure and slow his opponent.

He might not be as fast. He might not be as strong or subtle as his friends. But Daniel had two things they did not. Healing magic and a willingness to keep pushing, even through the pain he could not feel. It would just have to do, to win this battle.

***

Daniel staggered back, his chest heaving and feeling too tight under the breastplate with each too-warm inhalation. The stink of sweat and fear of spilled blood filled his nose with every hurried breath, warm blood dripping down one injured leg. His right hand hung limply by his side, the tendons in his elbow severed on the inside while he kept his shield arm high. A flush of warmth, a rumbling hunger ran through the Healer again as **Healer's Mark** triggered again, stitching wounds together. This was the third cast, and a part of him knew it would end soon.

All across the sandy training floor, splattered blood stained the earth. Deep gouge marks and a large depression where Daniel had unleashed **Perin's Blow** pitted the floor while his hammer, once picked up and then taken from him, lay outside the circle. Still, he had his shield, he had his Skill Proficiencies and he had still a portion of his Mana left. When Mana would take too long to heal, Daniel had his Gift.

Across from him, looking nearly as badly worn down as the Healer was the Rogue. His right eye was puffed up, bloody and swollen and impeding his vision out of it. Occasional blood dripped from the open scalp wound, forcing the Assassin to blink away the attack. That injury had come from a surprise **Double Strike** when Daniel had attempted a shield bash, taking a cut across his hip with the first attack and following up with his Skill the second time.

That was not the only wound the Rogue sported. His left hand barely held onto the dagger, the limb having been repeatedly struck by Daniel's armored and gauntleted arm, the nerves now afire and bruised. He limped around the healer slowly, toes on both feet crushed by repeated stamps. One side was favored; the glancing blow by **Perin's Blow** had cracked the Assassin's ribs.

The fight had slowed, both parties' endurance having drained over the intervening period. Daniel had lost track of time, the entirety of the fight seeming to have taken hours now subjectively, but he assumed it was only five or ten minutes. It felt a lot longer, but the constant pain and the application and purging of poisons he had been subjected to was leaving him light-headed.

In truth, he should have dropped by now. Blood loss if nothing else should have brought him to his knees. Instead, his Gift had even replaced that most precious of liquids. And all it had cost him was . . . *a soft hand on his face, a kiss . . . a conversation with his grandfather as they mined, together . . . the faces of his childhood friends, as they sorted the rocks searching for missed ore . . . a desperate battle as Imps came flocking up from under a bridge, swarming the group and tearing at them . . . walking along the road, as they journeyed to . . .*

Movement. Daniel brought his shield up, his other arm refusing to move properly. It jerked and twisted, but he ignored it as he caught the blade on the edge. It skipped off the top of his shield, striking the edge of his helmet, pushing him back a little.

Instinct took over. Push instead of retreat, tucking head and shoulders behind the shield. A pressure down near his hip, where the dagger that was coming to stick him glanced off armor, the Rogue's own control having suffered as well.

Impact, as Daniel pushed forward, caught fingers crushed against his opponent's own shoulder. He reeled back a little, and then slammed the boss of his shield into his opponent's face. Once, then again, **Double Strike** triggering. The loud crunching sound of nose being smashed, of spitting and teeth, of gurgled cries.

Head down, a foot was in sight. Crossing his leg behind it, Daniel hooked it towards himself as he stepped back, pulling his enemy's foot. Sudden loss of support turned into a smooth roll, and Daniel's stumbling pursuit caught up to the Rogue as he attempted to stand and failed, broken toes impeding his movements for a second.

Long enough for the edge of a shield to come down, cracking on collarbone. It shattered, forcing dagger to drop and driving his opponent to the ground, face down. Still, the Rogue managed to squirm around onto his back, just in time to get his sword in the way as Daniel dropped to his knees. A strangled squawk from his opponent beneath him as Daniel's armored knee came onto the tender flesh of the inner thigh.

The sword, without much space to swing, rang off his armor. Daniel struck with the edge of his shield again, driving the strike into the edge of his opponent's arm, catching it near the elbow. Fingers spasmed and the sword fell aside, moments later followed by Daniel as he let his greater weight and his armored form to collapse on his opponent, flattening him.

"Did they both die?" The queen's horrified voice rang out through the arena, cutting through the murmurs of disgust and admiration.

Lying on top of his opponent, Daniel just let himself relax rather than attempt to hold his opponent down. His weight and that of the armor was more than sufficient, and beneath him, his opponent was letting out harsh whimpers even as the healer tapped into his own Gift to properly fix his remaining arm. Then, knowing that the fight was nearly over, he used the last of his Mana to cast **Cure Medium Wounds** on himself.

"I do not think so. I think the healer is just resting and his opponent . . ." the king's voice grew troubled. "Might be unable to speak and give up. Master-of-Arms?"

"Yes, your majesty." Footsteps approached Daniel, even as the Master-of-Arms spoke. "Healer, please indicate you are still able to continue. If you do so, I shall rule this fight over in your favor."

There were a few murmured protests from the nobles, but not many. Most understood the likely outcome, and none wanted to see a promising youth die. Even if the promising youth's skills were less than savory.

"I can fight," Daniel said, his breathing having calmed a little. Stamina returned, he set one of his hands against the ground, shield still interspersed between himself and his opponent, and pushed himself to his knees a little.

To no one's surprise, his opponent did not surge forwards in a last valiant attempt at winning. Instead, he sucked in a hurried breath, his face red and filled with relief.

"It seems we have a winner, your majesty. The Adventurer Daniel Chai has won the final bout," the Master-of-Arms said phlegmatically before gesturing for the Healers to approach. Daniel, on his knees beside his opponent, waited for the rush of healing magic to hit him, only to realize none was forthcoming.

Staggering to his feet, Daniel turned his head as Healer Rotfield touched the nobleman, ignoring Daniel entirely after his first, cursory glance. Lips thinned, the Adventurer staggered away, a single thought running through his head as he returned to his cheering friends.

Rotfield was going to be a problem.

As his friends enveloped him in hugs, Daniel found himself smiling tiredly. At least, Rotfield and the nobles he'd shamed were going to be an issue for another day.

Today, they had won.

The End

Daniel and his friends will return for the ninth and final book of the Adventures on Brad series —
A Royal Ending

Epilogue

"Well?" Lady Marshall said, harshly.

Guildmaster Ronson flopped down on his chair, putting his feet up on his table. He flashed her a tired but victorious grin, as he tipped the chair back. "We did it."

Lady Marshall gave a little, unladylike whoop before she calmed herself and looked back at the shut door with suspicion. Seeing that it was still closed and no one was opening it, she walked over to the Guildmaster's drink cabinet and poured them both generous helpings of a smoky, dark liquor.

"Stealing my good stuff again?" Ronson good-naturedly grumbled, even as he reached forward to take the proffered glass.

"Seems like the right time for it, don't you think so?" Lady Marshall said. "So we got it all?"

"Yes. A royal member of the family as a member of our Guild and a noble family who'll owe us a favor," Ronson grinned savagely. "So long as you do your part for the last part."

"Relax, I'll make sure they think it's all their idea," Lady Marshall said with a grin.

Ronson smiled, nodding. "Of course. I trust you."

The pair laughed, toasting themselves once more and draining the glass before Ronson waved his empty glass. "More!"

"Now who's greedy?" Laughing, Lady Marshall stood and picked up the bottle, bringing it back. Their conversation turned to routine guild matters, spoken while the pair sipped on their alcohol.

And outside, Asin's ears twitched, the Catkin standing to her full height as she padded away silently. Her tail lashed out behind her languidly, a thoughtful look on her face as she crept off.

Author's Note:

Well, that's nearly the end of the Adventures on Brad. Daniel's story is coming to an end, at least in this arc. I hope you enjoy the conclusion as much as I do. The Adventures on Brad series was the first LitRPG I ever wrote and as such, holds a special place in my heart. Bringing Daniel to this point along with Asin has been a joy and I'm so grateful that you all have come along with me.

If you enjoyed reading the book, please leave a review and rating. Not only is it a big ego boost, it also helps sales and convinces me to write more in the series! Continue following Daniel's adventures in the next book:

- A Royal Ending

(Book 9 of the Adventures on Brad series)

https://books2read.com/u/38dler

Please check out my other series. I have written the System Apocalypse (a post-apocalyptic LitRPG), Adventures on Brad (a young adult fantasy LitRPG) and the Hidden Wishes (an urban fantasy GameLit). Book one of each series follow:

- Life in the North (Book 1 of the System Apocalypse)
  https://readerlinks.com/l/976138
- A Gamer's Wish (Book 1 of the Hidden Wishes series)
  https://books2read.com/gamers-wish
- A Thousand Li: the First Step (Book 1 of the A Thousand Li series)
  https://readerlinks.com/l/1340822

In addition, please take a look at other series/books I have co-written:

- Leveled up Love! by Tao Wong & A. G. Marshall
  https://books2read.com/u/3yexgZ
- A Fist Full of Credits by Tao Wong & Craig Hamilton (Book 1 of System Apocalypse: Relentless)
  https://readerlinks.com/l/2202673
- Town Under by Tao Wong & K.T. Hanna (Book 1 of System Apocalypse: Australia)
  https://readerlinks.com/l/2202672

For more great information about great LitRPG series, check out the Facebook groups:

- GameLit Society
  https://www.facebook.com/groups/LitRPGsociety
- LitRPG Books
  https://www.facebook.com/groups/LitRPG.books

And join my Cultivation Novel Group for more recommendations and to talk about the Thousand Li series.
https://www.facebook.com/groups/cultivationnovels

About the Author

Tao Wong is an avid fantasy and sci-fi reader who spends his time working and writing in the North of Canada. He's spent way too many years doing martial arts of many forms, and having broken himself too often, he now spends his time writing about fantasy worlds.

For updates on the series and other books written by Tao Wong (and special one-shot stories), please visit the author's website: http://www.mylifemytao.com

Or visit his Facebook Page:
https://www.facebook.com/taowongauthor

Subscribe to Tao's mailing list on his website to **receive exclusive access to short stories in the Thousand Li and System Apocalypse universes.**

About the Publisher

Starlit Publishing is wholly owned and operated by Tao Wong. It is a science fiction and fantasy publisher focused on the LitRPG & cultivation genres. Their focus is on promoting new, upcoming authors in the genre whose writing challenges the existing stereotypes while giving a rip-roaring good read.

For more information about latest releases and new, exciting authors from

Starlit Publishing, visit our website or sign up to our newsletter list:
https://www.starlitpublishing.com/

You can also join Starlit Publishing's mailing list to learn of new, exciting authors and book releases.